Stolen Virtue

A Virtuous Trilogy

Author Y. Deonna

Cover designed by Keri Knutson
https://www.alchemybookcovers.com/

Editor: Honey Berewa

Author Y. Deonna
Visit my website at authorydeonna.wixsite.com/crownedbythecreator

Printed in the United States of America

First Printing: April 2019

ISBN-13: 978-1-7330585-0-6

Dear Beloveds,
I dedicate this book series to all the victors and warriors who have survived physical, sexual and psychological abuse. Please understand that you're never alone; you're loved and you're His Beloved. I may not know your name or face, but I pray for all of you. Never give up, never lose faith and never forget that abuse isn't your fault. You're not a victim, but you're valuable, and you're a victor.
GET HELP
National Domestic Violence Hotline 1-800-799-SAFE
1-800-787-3224 (TTY)
National Center for Victims of Crime   1-855-484-2846

Author Note

<u>**This is not a standalone novel, but a trilogy and all books are complete!**</u>
Additionally, this series deals with traumatic issues, so if physical, psychological or sexual abuse are triggers or something you don't like to read then please pass on this one. This book is suggested <u>**for ages 17+**</u>. As always, thank you reader for your support. If you've enjoyed this read, then please leave a review on Amazon and/or Goodreads. I really appreciate and respect your reviews and constructive feedback!

Chapter 1

*V*irtuous, sat quietly in class, her youth instructor, Serena, lectured about something or the other. Her words had become as bothersome and pointless as Charlie Brown's teacher's *wompwomp*. It wasn't like Virtuous could concentrate anyway. Her mind was on what would happen after she left the church and who was waiting for her outside.

No one other than her legal guardians knew what she continuously suffered. It wasn't just the abuse. It was also the aftermath, the worthless feeling, the physical and mental agony, and the fear that another sin had been committed against her unwilling body, pulling her further from God. It was torture.

Some days, she implored God for death, only to turn around and beg God for forgiveness and ask Him to set her free.

Free... She supposed freedom, the beautiful seven-letter word, would forever be beyond her reach. But in her mind, she was a black tigress ruling her queendom, an alter-ego she had created to withstand the abuse of the man she called

Father, the man who had stolen her virtue. He was a man she loved and loathed. Their relationship was indeed a paradox that often had her perplexed and full of self-hate. She loved him because he was the only father she knew, but she loathed him because he constantly abused his power as a father. He was the cause of everything that was bad in her life. Removing the thoughts, she traveled deeper into her fictitious world of utopia where she banished all negativity and all hurt. Pain couldn't enter here. This was a safe space, her *World of All*. This was where she ruled, but unlike Greg, she was a gracious and kind ruler.

"Vivi, what do you think?" Serena queried.

However, Virtuous was already deeply enrooted into her other world, completely disassociated. It was the only way she knew how to cope, and it was no bleeding over into her everyday life. She had to get a hold on it.

"Vivi!" Tamari, her best and only friend, shook her, causing Virtuous to re-enter reality.

Virtuous glanced around flummoxed and saw a rainbow of eyes looking her way, waiting for what she suspected was a response, but to what, she had no clue.

Sensing her dilemma Serena simply nodded and let it be. It wasn't the first time Virtuous had drifted like this nor would it be the last. Her mind was always plagued and full of worry.

Once they were dismissed, Tamari pulled Virtuous aside, causing her to frown. If she were late, Greg would suspect she was talking to boys or making plans without his consent and then she'd have to hear him drone on about rules and why she needed to follow his.

"What's up?" Tamari queried.

Tamari was just like her law-enforcement father. She could smell a situation a mile away, and since they were close friends, Tamari could always pick up on Virtuous' mood swings. As badly as Virtuous wanted to confide in her best friend what she was enduring at home, she stayed silent. No one wanted to carry that burden, and secondary trauma was real, so she couldn't do that to Tamari.

"Nothing. I've just been tired. With my siblings, helping around the house, and trying to maintain a high-grade point average, I guess I just drifted. It happens." Virtuous shrugged her shoulders indifferently. It was a lie and she prayed that God wouldn't smite her for it, but the truth was explosive. At this point in her life, *lies* were the truth.

"It does. Lately, you haven't been yourself, you know. Like after you got sick last year and had to do homebound, it's like you never bounced back. I'm worried, but I'm your best friend, so if something was wrong, you'd tell me," Tamari confidently declared.

Instead of saying anything, Virtuous simply embraced her best friend and then told her goodbye.

Two weeks later...

Virtuous' body trembled at the abuse it had just received. This was the aftermath of madness, *his* madness marking his territory like she was nothing more than property. It was a reminder that she belonged to him because she had made the mistake of speaking to her cousin and his friends. She didn't even cry anymore because there wasn't any need to do so. He was unaffected by tears and had been since he started taking her at his will.

Long ago, her teenage body had stopped belonging to her and started belonging to him. There was little she could do about it because no one would ever believe her word against his. So, she went to her safe space, her *World of All*. The reality was that she was trapped, scared, and lonely. It was the way Greg wanted it to be. She was easier to manage when she didn't have a support group.

Virtuous' head turned slightly as she heard the shuffling of Greg's footfalls and she presumed he had sauntered into the en suite bathroom to take care of his hygiene. Greg's tall semi-massive toasted alabaster frame stood so unimposingly, but she knew the monster lurking in the man and just how uncontrolled he could become. She'd seen all sides of him. Closing her eyes to calm her battered body, her short slumber was interrupted as he returned with a washcloth to clean her up. She didn't refuse him or wince as he touched her soreness. She just took it. That seemed like the theme of her life: *Just take it*.

He spoke unromantic words, something about her being good and soft and how he loved her body, but she didn't really care. All she wanted to do was go back to her own bedroom that she shared with her sisters, but he wanted pillow talk now and she had nothing to say. Shaking her head, she wondered how she'd gotten here and would she ever get away. Would she ever know freedom or love?

Virtuous was born in the autumn of 1998 with a fraternal twin, Valor All. She and her brother were abandoned at a church, never to see or know their biological parents. They were separated at a young age, so young that most would think she didn't remember him, but she did. She never saw Valor again, but in her heart, she knew he was out there somewhere. It was her prayer that her brother was fairing far better than her.

All she knew was Greg, her legal guardian and father for all purposes had been using her body as his own entertainment since she was thirteen-years-old. *Thirteen!* She hated that unlucky number and she hated how Greg used her at his will to do whatever he wanted whenever he wanted.

The wailing of the baby sucked her back to reality and out of her reverie. How she despised reality and apparently, so did Greg, but for different reasons. She heard him complain, signaling that he didn't care for the interruption. As much as she hated reality, she was glad to hear the baby crying because that meant she could leave. Even though he violated her at every turn, Greg seemed to love the girls, Tory, who was about to be a year old, and Maddison, who was seven. They were his biological children. Both girls were sweet as could be. It was Greg's nephew through marriage, Jason, who he had adopted, that sometimes concerned her. He was Greg's eyes and ears.

"I better go check on Tory." Virtuous' voice whispered. Every part of her body yearned to push him off, stomp him into oblivion, and then ask him how he liked having another control his body. She kept those thoughts and actions to herself like she kept so many secrets, dreams, and prayers. It would do her no good to incite his rage. Instead, she simply said a prayer and asked God to remember her. Lately, she wasn't sure if He even heard her pleas of desperation, but if she allowed herself to believe that God had closed His ears to her, then she would become hopeless and being hopeless was dangerous.

Greg rolled off her, resting his hand on the side her face, taking her all in as if she were his last meal. It always made her uncomfortable when he looked at her like that. Finally, he spoke, giving her the words, she longed to hear. "Yeah, go ahead. Addison should be back soon, and she might not appreciate us making love in the bed. I'll change the sheets and you go check on my girls."

Virtuous nodded and quickly slipped back on her nightgown and somberly ambled back to her bedroom. She knew that Tory was crying because she'd woken up and Virtuous wasn't there to hold her. Since Addison was a functioning addict, Virtuous stepped into the role of mom. Addison was neglectful, which was crazy because she was a registered nurse and Greg was a police officer. They were active in their church.

The family looked so flawless on the outside, but they were coming apart at the seams. That's what Virtuous wanted to confess to Tamari, Serena, and anyone who would listen, but didn't. Well, it was more like she *couldn't*. To the outside world, they looked like a typical middle-class family, but that was far from the truth. This family was everything God wasn't.

As faithful to God as Virtuous was, her faith was being tested daily and she wasn't sure how much more she could take. If God was omnipotent, omniscient, and omnipresent, then where was He now? Where were her guardian angels? Where was her escape? Had God left her when Greg stole her virtue or had He abandoned her the same night as her biological parents?

There was never an answer, only theories, but they only led to worry. The Bible said not to worry. However, what was she supposed to do when her prayers went unanswered?

Erasing the invasive thoughts, she entered her bedroom and went to Tory. Just like that, Virtuous shifted and went into protective mode. As soon as she grabbed the baby, her sobbing stopped, and out of habit, Virtuous sang to her as she changed her diaper and then trotted over to check on Maddison who was still fast asleep. *Good.* The two of them together could be a monumental task to soothe. At least they had the day off.

Today, rather, later today, was a teacher in-service day, so the children didn't have school and she needed to find a way to keep the little ones occupied. A few seconds later, Tory was asleep again and Virtuous laid her down and just snuggled with her. She loved the smell innocence and hope. The organic baby lotion made Tory softer than rose petals. It was Tory who helped her not to fall completely in to the awaiting abyss of hopelessness. When her *World of All* failed her, she thought of the girls.

It only felt like seconds, but she was sure it was at least an hour when Virtuous was awakened by a loud noise. Instantly, fear began to seep through her marrow. Muffled voices alerted her that another intimate-partner violence situation between Greg and Addison was about to ensue.

This was a regular occurrence that had worsened over the years. Greg despised that Addison was a pill popper and she loathed that he preferred having an intimate relationship with a girl he had legal guardianship over. However, Virtuous knew for a fact that Addison had another lover, but that wasn't her business to share.

When Virtuous heard the shattering of glass she jumped up and went to see if she could de-escalate the situation. Maddison could sleep through anything, but not Tory or Jason. Virtuous didn't want either of them to wake up and witness this maelstrom. She had faith in herself that she'd be able to solve the issue.

With shaky confidence, she sprinted to the master bedroom only to find it empty. So, she ran downstairs and followed the trail of blood that ended in the dining room where Addison was balled into the fetal position and Greg was standing over her.

Greg's face was evil, reminding her of an aggressive pit bull prepared to attack its prey to death. The sharp insults he slung at Addison were vile, insensitive, and unforgiving, making Virtuous feel sorrowful for her. Then to her shock, Greg lifted his bat to strike Addison. It looked like he'd already done it several times by the red whelps that were developing on her pale skin.

The whacking sound made Virtuous draw into herself, triggering past trauma, but she quickly regained her senses. "Daddy, stop!" Virtuous pleaded. She didn't call him that easily, but it was a rule. You didn't break Greg's rules. Everybody called him Daddy, including Addison at times.

His left hand froze like a statue in the air, and slowly and ever so easily, Virtuous ambled cautiously over, making sure not to make any sudden movements. He was in that space, the scary place where nothing could reach him, but her. "Daddy, I'm going to help Mom up and take her to the bedroom to sleep it off. Is that okay?"

Greg glowered at Addison, hate easy to read in his eyes, but he lowered the bat. "You're a disgrace, Addy! I swear I shouldn't have ever married you. You can't give me any more children because your womb is all tore up. You stumble around like a meth zombie and when that ain't enough, you're popping pills. You ain't nothing but a Walmart-version of Nurse Jackie."

Virtuous could see this going downhill from here. Addison carefully unfolded her languid body at Virtuous' coaxing. Her hair was plastered to her face with a mixture of tears and sweat holding her strands captive. Her skin, though damp, had a gray hue to it, possibly from her drug abuse or her lack of taking care of herself. However, what gave Virtuous pause was the murky murderous look in her cold eyes, like she had reached that level of enough. Every other part of her body spoke weak, sick, and strain, but her eyes spoke resolve, rage, and revenge. It was as if she wanted to fight back against the monster that had been in power for as long as Virtuous could remember.

"Don't," Virtuous implored desperately, but either the drugs or adrenaline were pumping because Addison leaped like a gazelle and pounced like a lioness protecting her cubs, attacking not Greg who had just beat her like an Old Testament Hebrew slave, but she attacked *Virtuous*, screaming she abhorred her.

"Get off me!" Virtuous demanded, not understanding why Addison had chosen to abuse her. The woman had the strength of five armies. For some reason, people on drugs seemed to have super-human strength. Finally, Greg yanked Addison off her, but she was still slanging insults. Both she and Virtuous were breathing heavily.

"I hate you, Virtuous! Nothing about your slutty ways is virtuous. You stole him from me! He loved me until you put some voodoo on him! I want my life back! You're a home wrecker!" Addison screamed violently, pointing her index finger with force to drive home the insult.

That took Virtuous aback, seeing that she did not want to be in their home from the start. She would do just about anything to have Greg leave her alone. There was nothing about her dad that she found attractive. It was her hope he would lose interest. Furthermore, if Addison was so outraged, then she should have turned Greg in a long time ago, but instead, she'd let him rape Virtuous at his will. The home wrecker was *Greg*, not her.

"Go back to bed, Virtue. I'll handle this." Greg seethed, turning soulless eyes on his wife who shut up when he glared at her.

"I'm sorry that you detest me, Addison. I never wanted–"

"Hush and go to bed like I said, Virtuous. Don't be rude. Do as Daddy has asked you." He gave her a pointed glare that told her the conversation was over and that she better do as she'd been told.

Virtuous nodded and left the two to their own devices. She chastised herself for attempting to appease Addison when she was just as guilty as Greg. Just because she didn't sexually assault her didn't absolve her of guilt. "God save me, please," she mumbled for only herself to hear.

A & Ω

Greg looked at Addison's face in disgust. He just couldn't stand her, and tonight was the last straw. He wanted her gone. There was nothing beautiful about her anymore. She was a pill popper and an adulteress. He knew all about her dating the white Hispanic tech at the hospital where she worked. He had long lost interest in her. As a matter of fact, their marriage was a complete sham. Well, it was now. He was just holding on for appearances.

Addison used to be an attractive woman who had goals and aspirations. They'd met in college. Back then, he was studying criminal justice and she was working on her BSN. She was bright, witty, and there was a glow about her. She had the prettiest strawberry-blonde hair and she always smelt like strawberries. She was a good girl with that perfect milky complexion, and he was smitten.

She'd always talked about fostering or adopting, so he was fine with that if she agreed to have at least one child for him. She had readily agreed. He didn't know at the time they would have difficulty conceiving. Anyway, their first child was Virtuous. She was so young when she came to them. She was a beautiful little girl and he immediately fell in love with her. He took her everywhere. And then came Jason, his nephew by marriage. He was a troubled kid early on and his mom, Beatrice, Addy's middle sister, couldn't handle him, so she gave him up and ran off. Then, a few years later, his wife's womb decided it wanted to work and they had Maddison. During that time, Greg fell out of love with his wife. She was on and off drugs, but after having Maddison, she became a full-time abuser. Maybe it was post-partum depression. Greg did not know and no longer cared.

There was sweet Virtuous who'd taken to becoming a mom far better than Addy. As she grew older, her body filled out so nicely that he couldn't help but sample her and that was all it was supposed to have been. He'd had no intention of falling for Virtuous, but he had. By no means was he a child molester or pedophile. He had just fallen in love with someone who was twenty-three years younger than him. Virtuous was his addiction and he wasn't ashamed. Now, he was at a crossroad. There was no way he could let Addy hurt Virtuous. She was *his*. Bottom line, if he had to choose between his wife and Virtuous, he would always choose Virtuous.

"Get up, Addy!"

She did, but she was all dramatic with it and whimpering like she was hurt. All that fight that was in her when she was attacking *his* Virtuous was gone. He was going to make Addy pay for that too. It was Virtuous who went to school and then came home to clean the house, take care of the kids, and cook. Addy didn't do anything but sleep and do drugs. She functioned, but not at the level she used too, and she had taken to coming home late at night smelling like another man. Then she wanted to argue with him because he was doing the same. *What kinda sense did that make?*

"Why, Greg? I'm good to you. I can get clean."

"No, you're toxic to me and the children. You had no right to hit Virtuous. Don't you *ever* touch her!" he fumed. How dare she attempt to scar Virtuous' unblemished skin? Virtuous was perfect in his mind. She was tall, slender, curvy with golden skin, and hazel eyes. Her body had been created to accommodate his.

"We can make it work. I'm sorry. I'll do better. I promise!" she pleaded, eyes widened in fear.

Greg didn't understand at first and then he realized at some point he had exchanged his bat for his gun. Addison was pleading for her life. He wouldn't waste a bullet on her. He wanted her out of his life, but she would not die by his hand at least not tonight. "You're sorry, but we can't make this work. Let this be the last time you ever attack my Virtuous. I know about your little boyfriend. You can keep him because I'll never touch you again. You're no longer fit to be in this family. You have two choices. You can leave now and never come back or you can get beaten every day and watch as Virtuous enjoys the life you used to have. *I don't want you!* I love Virtuous and so do the kids. Even your nephew prefers her to you." He sneered cruelly. He truly detested Addy for what she had made him do to Virtuous back when she was just thirteen. It was all *her* fault that he had turned to his daughter for comfort.

Tears streamed down Addison's face, but Greg remained unaffected. Tears did nothing for him. "Make a decision right now."

"I'll go, Greg. Just please don't hit me anymore and don't shoot me."

"Good. Leave *now*. I'll have someone send your belongings. I want you out of my house. Don't contact anyone who lives here. My lawyer will notify you soon. We're divorcing, and I'll have full custody of the children, and you're not getting any spousal support. Understand?"

She nodded as best she could since he had a gorilla grip on her.

"Great. Now, give me the keys to my house and you can be on your way."

With shaking fingers, Addison handed Greg the keys and he took off the ones he needed before handing them back. He helped her up and escorted her from the house. He watched her leave and let out a sigh of relief.

He closed the door, locked it, and turned the security system on again. When he turned around, he saw Virtuous standing there in her little nightgown. Just seeing her tamed his temper. "I thought I told you to go to bed."

"I did, but Tory was hungry. I was just getting her a snack. That's all. Virtuous dropped her head, more than likely thinking she was in trouble. He never had to be violent with her because she knew her place. She did whatever she was told.

"Once you've fed her, come back to our bed. Addy has left us, and we've agreed to get a divorce. That means you're the woman in charge now. No more sneaking around. I can kiss you and hold you whenever I want," he cooed.

"Um, okay. I better feed Tory." Then she zoomed away, leaving a perplexed Greg. Maybe she was still in a daze after Addy attacked her. Shaking his head, he began the clean. He didn't want his young daughters to see the blood or the mess.

One hour later, Greg was done cleaning and went searching for Virtuous and found her sitting on their bed reading the Bible. His Virtuous was serious about her Bible reading and as well as reading it to the girls. He was sure Maddison and Tory would make it to heaven because of the strong values she was instilling in them. Even he enjoyed attending church with Virtuous. She was active with the children's ministry and a lot of people admired his family because of it.

"Baby, it's four in the morning. Let's sleep and when we wake up, we can spend the day in Gaffney at the Prime Outlet and take the kids to the Big E for some fun. We got lots to celebrate."

"Okay. That's good because Maddison needs some new shoes."

Her response was dull, which caused him to look up at her and frown. "Baby, what's wrong?"

"Nothing is wrong. I was just reading is all."

He felt like it was something more, but sometimes, she got in her little ways and he let it be. "Put the Bible away and show me some attention now. I want to cuddle. This morning has been an ordeal and I need you to relax me."

She promptly did as he'd requested and turned off the lamp before allowing her body to be pulled into his. "I love you, Virtuous. Nothing can come between us now. You're mine forever." He felt her shiver in his embrace and held her tighter, thinking she was cold, but that wasn't it. She was terrified.

Chapter 2

Theory 'Vicious' Campbell was a free man. He had been locked up so long that he didn't even know what freedom was. He was fifteen when he'd gotten locked up for robbery and a weapons charge. He was lucky they hadn't added murder to his charges or try him as an adult since the lady he'd robbed had suffered a heart attack and later died. He still didn't know how that'd worked out for him. His grandmother was a praying woman, so God must have heard her. A black man robbing a white lady and said lady died in the state of South Carolina, well yeah, there was indeed a God.

Theory had never been so happy in his entire life and when he saw his little cousin, Val, with their grandma, Naomi, he was too ecstatic. Juvie hadn't hardened his heart. If anything, it had taught him how good he'd had it on the outside. His grandmother and cousin wouldn't allow him to become bitter and belligerent. It had changed his entire outlook on life. Thank God for them because things could have been far worse. "Val, what it do?" Theory shouted as he ran to him.

Val was like a little brother to him. They had been raised by their grandparents after Val's mom, Sherry, had gotten caught up in a prostitution ring and his military father, Uncle Gerald, had abandoned the family. One day little Val had shown up at Grammy and Pop's house and the two instantly became best friends. He knew Val had taken it hard after his dad left him, but Uncle Gerald just wasn't right after coming back from Afghanistan. At least that's what he had heard the grown folks say.

"Nothing much going on, Theo. Man, am I happy to see you." Val grinned, embracing him like he hadn't just seen him just two days ago.

Theory laughed at being called Theo. Neither his Grammy nor Val ever referred to him by his street moniker. Maybe that was for the best. Maybe he needed to leave the Vicious persona in juvie because he wasn't that person anymore and he wasn't going back to the street life. He was just Theory Correion Campbell or Theo.

"Come here and let me love on you, baby," their grandmother crooned. Theory adored her. He hated what he had put her through, but as a kid, he was full of rabid rage. It was rage at his parents, his lack of financial income, the death of his grandfather, and just life. Sadly, he'd fallen into the wrong crowd, but he was glad Naomi no longer lived in Anderson. She and Val had relocated to Spartanburg a.k.a. *Sparkle City* and Val was finishing up his senior year in high school. He was an amazing athlete and academician.

Val had confided in Theory that he didn't know if he should stay in state or go out of state since some of the big-named universities and even the United States Naval Academy wanted him for his talent and intellect. That made Theory proud.

Val wasn't as muscular as Theory, but for seventeen, he was built, and the boy had been in sports since he'd come to live with them. He played soccer, football, track, and baseball. He was a good swimmer too. That had been Grammy's way of keeping them out of the streets. It'd worked for Val, but not for Theory. He thought *thugging* was the life until it got him locked up. His grandmother had put him out the house because he had failed to do right, and she was scared he would infect Val with his poisonous ways.

That had led to Theory's wayward life of crime. He wasn't built to be a corner boy, but he'd partaken part in being a stick-up kid and he could fight, which saved him many of times, especially in juvie.

Clearing his thoughts, he fell into Grammy's embrace. She still smelled sweet like pound cake, sweet potatoes and, confectioner's sugar. He loved the scent because it felt like home, comfort, and safety.

Grammy was barely 5'5", so he towered over her at 6'2" plus he was built. So, his grandmother disappeared into his arms, but you could best believe the little lady ruled with an iron fist when needed. "I'm sorry, Grammy. I won't ever do anything stupid like that again."

"I know, baby. C'mon and get in the car. We got a big surprise for you back at the house."

He smiled, kissed her cheek, and got into the car.

A little while later, they pulled up at a house, which was located down the street from a local college where his grandmother wanted him to apply to, so he could at least get his Associate's degree. He was twenty-one and he had graduated high school while locked up and he'd done well. He was for sure going to college. He would do anything Naomi asked of him after what he had put her through.

The house wasn't much to brag about on the outside to most people, but to Theo, it was a mansion after being in juvie for so long. He was just glad that his little cousin hadn't gotten caught up like he had. Nearly half a decade ago, he had thought he knew everything, but now, he realized just how dumb he was. His vicious spirit had gotten him caught up, but he'd learned his lesson and he would never be the person he used to be.

As soon as he opened the passenger's door, everybody flooded out of the house. His aunts, uncles, other cousins, and some old friends from back in Anderson were there. Grammy had given birth to six children who were all boys. Only two were missing: Val's father, Gerald, and Theory's father, Stanley. Theory still had lots of family. He smiled at their love and support. He mentally berated himself for not seeing this before.

Back in the day, he had a chip on his shoulder. His parents were drug addicts. The drugs had started off being for recreational purposes, but then they got hook so badly that his parents sold him to their dealer. Like, who does that? After that, Grammy and Pops took him in to raise him. He was barely four then and had the battle scars of a man in war.

His parents had been neglectful and abusive. If it hadn't been for Grammy, he would've probably been an addict or dead.

"Vicious, man, it's good to see you. Dang, you done got big, strutting around here all swollen, looking like a hot-air balloon," Archie teased before giving him a man hug and dapping him.

Arlando 'Archie' Cannon was 6'0" and pushing two hundred and thirty pounds. His complexion was a mixture of peach and butterscotch, which had earned him the childhood nickname Yella, although he had outgrown that nickname and had taken to being called Archie instead. He was one loyal dude. They often cracked on each other, even when Archie had gone to visit him. That was just Archie. He used humor to deal.

"Archie, I see you got jokes, but you about to need some oxygen just walking two feet. Pace yourself, Ole Yella, over here wobbling like a penguin. Bruh, you like two pounds from being on that show "My 600-Pound Life.""

"Okay, I see how it is." Archie chortled as Theory was greeted by the rest of his family.

Theory finally made it inside the house and Val showed him where his bedroom was. He wasn't surprised at how clean the house was. Grammy didn't play about her home. It was bigger than he had expected and when he entered his very own bedroom, the tears welled up in his eyes. Even at their old house he and Val had shared a bedroom, but this was nice. It smelled Pine-Sol clean. He meandered to the closet and saw he had new clothes and shoes.

"I work at the shoe store in the mall and some of your boys bought you some clothes, but I got all the shoes. I know how you love your shoes," Val told him, grinning.

Theory turned around, tears falling because of the outpouring of love he had received after he'd cut up so bad. He hugged his little cousin. "Thanks, bruh. You were really looking out for ya boy. I'm so proud of you. You on the honor roll, probably getting a full scholarship to any college you want, and you got a job. You're goals, baby boy. You know that. I love you, dude."

"Cool all that mushy mess. We're family. You're my brother and that's what family does. We look out for each other. Now, take a shower, change your clothes, and then come back out. We got you a surprise or two." Val turned to leave and as if having a second thought, he turned around with his signature grin and spoke, "I love you too, big head." Then he left.

Theory took in a deep breath and just looked around his bedroom. It was nice, he thought. This was the surprise. He dropped his head and cried, like a real soul-cleansing cry and he thanked God. He got down on his knees and said a prayer of thanksgiving.

After a moment with God, he got up. Val was right. He needed to wash juvie off him. He went to shower. It felt so good to have hot water and not to have to see other males, so he could finally let his guard down and he did.

Thirty minutes later, his body and mouth were clean. He dressed up in a Polo shirt and Levi jeans. It had to have been Archie who got the clothes, 'cause Vicious was a jersey and jogging pants kind of dude, but his shoe game was tight. Val had hooked him up, so for the outfit he chose some wheat Timberlands. Val had every color in the closet, but he was feeling old school.

Theory brushed his hair. He had silky curls, courtesy of his mother. He had that fine grain of hair like Russell Wilson. He took a moment and looked at himself in the mirror. He looked fresh and handsome. He stood 6'2" and weighed two hundred and fifteen pounds, nothing but muscle. Theory's brown eyes were outlined by thick U-curled lashes and his eyebrows were thin and perfectly arched on their own. He hated that, but the ladies liked it. The only spot on his face was a chicken pox scar. Other than that, his face was unscarred and clean shaven. He had what some described as a button nose, but it fit his face. He reached for the organic shea butter and rubbed it between his hands to moisturize his face and neck. Yeah, he was a bit of a pretty boy.

"What are you doing, Theo? Grammy said c'mon. She wants you to see your surprises."

"I'm checking out all this fineness."

"Bruh, please, everybody knows I'm the fine one. I'm taller than you by two inches, I got the sandy skin, hazel eyes, and honey-blonde hair. The chicks dig me, bruh. I'm sorry to break it to you, but I'm the finest one in this family. You are number two!" he teased.

Theory guffawed. "You better tell the truth and shame the devil. The women love this smooth, butta-brown skin and soft curls," he told him and placed his arm around his neck before they strolled outside where their Uncle Clyde was manning the grill and his other cousin, Trek, was deejaying.

"Here ya go, son. The family pulled together and gotcha this," Luther, his other uncle, stated as he tossed some keys on the table.

"What's this?"

"Go and see," Luther instructed.

Theory did and Val followed, him videotaping him with his iPhone 6, which he was learning how to use on the ride home. When he got to the front yard again, there was a 2015 Chevrolet Colorado 4WD Z71truck. All the woman came out of him. He screamed, jumped, and went running to the truck like he was on The Price Is Right. He opened the door and almost had a fit. Inside was a box with a pure black pit bull puppy. He knew his grandma had gotten it for him because the one his father had gotten him had died. He had to grab his heart to try and control the beating and his breathing.

"This me?" he queried, trying to hide his elation.

Grammy just smiled. "Yes. Luther works at the car dealership, so he got a good deal on it and it's all paid for. I got you that puppy 'cause I know you wanted another one. You know your brother and your friends hooked up your clothes and shoes. All you got to do is go to school and graduate. Think of this as all of the Christmases and birthdays we never got to celebrate with you."

"Thank y'all," Theory replied humbly as he hugged his gram and uncle. Theory was just so overtaken by emotions. He had expected nothing and had come home to be treated like a king. God knew he was blessed and come Sunday, you could best believe he was going to Sunday school and church no matter how long it lasted. He knew that God was offering him a second chance at being a better man and he was determined to do just that.

After the mini celebration, everybody went to the backyard to eat. Theory was piling enough food on his plate to rival Archie, which was saying something because homeboy could eat. That was his brother from another mother, so it was all love.

Just as he reclaimed his seat, a group of chicks arrived. Two of them had that stereotypical hood-chick look with bizarre nails. One was rocking purple hair and the other royal blue. They had some twisted braids, but he didn't know what they were called. Then there was the one who looked like her stuff didn't stink, and the other two looked like sisters. They were cute and had butts that K. Michelle would envy. They looked kind of familiar.

"Val, who them chicks?"

Val gave him an incredulous look like he was supposed to know who they were. "Well, two of them are your cousins, Rika and Maisha. They're the ones with butt for days. Grammy said it's the cornbread and collards that got 'em."

"What? Them Clyde's daughters?" he queried in shock. When had they developed like that? He instantly felt disgusted with himself.

"Yep, now the uppity-looking one is Nora Jean. We call her No cause that's all she says. The hood twins are Celina and Deandrea, but they're not really twins or even kin. At least I don't think so. I just call them that because they dress similarly. Fair warning, stay away from all three of them 'cause they messy and thirsty. I'm talking like desert thirst. Call them chicks Gobi. You know that desert in Asia 'cause they're that dehydrated for some male attention."

Theory threw his head back laughing until tears fell from his eyes. Hearing proper Val speak like that and throw shade was too funny. He had been around Archie too long. Val had been raised in the hood like him, but he didn't talk or act like it. One would never know of his humble background, but dudes wouldn't test Val because he had them hands. Theory had made sure of that. Nobody was going to come for his little cousin.

"Archie said he gonna take you to the club this weekend, so if you can hold off, I say do that. Rika and Maisha's three home girls ain't what you want. I think one of them got a baby. All they're doing is sponsor shopping except Nora Jean. You got to have a certain amount of bread to be her benefactor. She's probably here for the free food, though.

"She's an EBT-card-carrying gold digger at eighteen. I mean I'm not knocking her hustle, but really, get a job, not a man. All of them ain't nothing but Dollar Store chotties. Grammy says it ain't nice to call women thotties or THOT's, so I call them CHOT's, also known as church harlots out there. It sounds less offensive."

Theory's food shot out of his mouth. He wasn't ready for that. He literally almost died. "Bruh, I just got out, so don't make me flatline while I'm tryna eat. Only you would come up with something like that."

"What? What I say?" he questioned innocently, which made it even funnier.

"You're doing too much right now, but I'm glad to know that your whore-oculars are on point and updated. Thanks for letting me know."

"No problem. Aw, man, here comes Jem and the Hoegrams. I meant the *Holograms*, cousins included," Val corrected.

This time Theory wasn't eating, but he did almost choke on his sweet iced tea. Val was on high alert right now. Theory was trying to get himself together, and Val's crazy self was patting him on his back like that was helping. By the time he finished, the girls had arrived.

"Hey, cuzzo!" Rika and Maisha cooed at the same time. Their bright brown eyes and welcoming smile gave them an innocence that their friends didn't have.

He smiled and parroted the greeting.

"Well, we're glad you remember us. Daddy wouldn't let us visit you. I see Uncle Luther got you a new ride."

"Yeah. Honestly, I didn't remember y'all. When I got locked up y'all were rocking pigtails and sandals."

"Yep, now they got CHOT dots, tramp stamps, baby daddies, and disabled edges. It's a hard-knock life," Val chimed in with a serious expression before he took a bite out of his rib, making half of the table erupt in laughter, Theory included. However, the girls frowned and sucked their teeth. Theory was close to tears again. Val was doing the most right now and he wasn't prepared for the sarcasm and jokes that were freely flowing. Val hadn't been anything like this when

Theory caught his case. He liked this laid-back, fast-to-crack Val. He was entertaining.

"Real cute, Velour," Maisha snapped. "FYI, I got my edges and no baby daddy or a tramp stamp," Maisha replied sarcastically, balling up her face and jumping at Val like she was going to beat him up.

Val proceeded to lick the sauce off his fingers completely unbothered. "It's Valor Noble Campbell and notice how she didn't deny she's a CHOT, Theo. I told you she was out here being reckless. She's sitting up in Sunday school sending PG-13 pics to the pastor's son, acting like she's the long-lost member of the Greenleaf family. When Unc finds you, she'll be singing *locked up, he won't let me out.*" Again, there was laughter.

"Lies you tell and anyway, you ain't nobody special looking like an albino Gumby. You got one little blonde hair under your chin and think you grown," Maisha insulted.

"Wait. You mean that green clay thing with the slanted head? I can't, an albino Gumby. Val, she just gotchu." Archie laughed and Maisha smirked, satisfied. That didn't slow down Val or his comeback.

"You're looking like a Black Velma Dinkley. Where Scooby Doo and the Mystery Machine at? I swear ever since you got colored contacts, found them makeup tutorials on YouTube, and relaxed that natural hair, you out here trying to turn up and talk smack. Anyhow, this is a family gathering, but you dressed like you at the club. Who are you trying to impress? Out here looking like Stephen King's "It" with all that makeup on!" Valor shot back.

Theory was redder than a stop sign from laughing so hard. His entire body shook. "Stop it! Y'all got my stomach cramping."

"Val, you're as vicious as Theory. Mai, you lost that round. You know what's real funny? You really are wearing the same colors and that cartoon character Velma." Archie interjected shaking his head. "He said you look like "It." I'm done!"

Rika ignored the entire side conversation and kept her attention on Theory like her sister hadn't just gotten schooled by Val. "True, we were babies. Well, anyway, let me introduce you to my friends. This is Nora Jean."

"Just Nora," Nora interrupted as if Theory cared, but he just nodded. He was concerned about his cousins. Honestly, he never thought his cousins would be like that since they were all raised in the church and Rika and Maisha were good girls. Somebody must have turned them out and when he found out who it was, he was cracking faces. After Sherry's downfall into that dark world, he didn't think the girls would follow down that path.

"This is Celina and Deandrea. They're in high school with me, but Nora attends community college with Maisha. Y'all, this is Vicious," Rika finished.

Good. Now, he knew for a fact he wasn't attending community college with them. "Well, it's nice to meet y'all. Val was just telling me 'bout you ladies. If you'd excuse us, I'd like to spend time with Grammy. Val and Archie, y'all enjoy yourselves."

Theory saw the attitude clouding all their faces. He wasn't even down for it. Two seconds of watching the three chicks eat him up with their eyes let him know what they were about. He wasn't even trying to have a girl, and whenever he did, she was going to be an educated sister, not some lollipop sucking, 3-D-weave-wearing girl, putting an APB out for her edges from the projects whose only goal in life was to find a benefactor to take care of her. He wasn't desperate for that kind of female. No, he wasn't hating on girls from the hood or the projects because it was where he'd come from. He was hating on girls who didn't respect themselves or their temples. He was on another level now. He wanted a woman who put God first, not her thirst.

As they turned from the table, he heard the one name Nora disrespect him, talking about he wasn't that cute, and he ought to have been happy they had even come to his welcome-home party. Now, the new Theory wanted to chill and let bygones be bygones, but seriously, he wasn't there yet. He was going to keep his response respectful since his Grammy was right beside him.

"Yo," Theory called out, his deep baritone thundered over the music. He stood up and smoothed out his outfit, which he felt gave off the preppy-boy look when he was anything but. "Nora, is it?"

She turned and smiled at him. Never trust a chick that changed it up that quick. This chick had some bipolar tendencies. Theory knew for sure that Nora was one of them burn-your-house-down chicks. "It is," she replied sassily like that was sexy. *Not*. Even though he'd been locked up for a minute, her antics didn't turn him on even a little bit.

"Listen up, my cousins, Rika and Maisha, know me and they know I have zero patience for stupidity and lame disses. You're mad because you sought some attention from me that I won't ever give you. I suggest you find a quieter way to deal with the rejection. Secondly, this is *my* home, not yours. So, don't come to a house you were invited to and show out 'cause you can get put out. I just got released and I really don't need to catch another case, but if you don't check your attitude, please believe I will. So, you'll apologize for that disrespectful banter that I overheard. You'll apologize not only to me but to my family as well and then you'll leave."

Her mouth dropped so wide that an entire family of flies could've zoomed in. To make matters worse, her so-called girls were laughing at her. Yup, Theory was dead serious. He also noticed how quiet it had become because his family knew how he was. He didn't play even a little bit.

"He's waiting!" Archie instigated.

"I'm sorry. I apologize to all of you," she said and huffed. She was big mad, but what could she do?

"Good. Now, you can go," he told her and turned away.

"Theory, you know you wrong. You supposed to let her take a doggie bag home. You know she came here for a free meal. Dang, now, she's going to be hungry *and* lonely," Archie joked.

Theory shrugged his shoulders and went back to his food, and Val was killing himself laughing as Nora Jean turned and left alone.

Theory turned to his grandmother to apologize, but she was laughing too. "I'm glad she's gone. Now, I don't have to ask her to leave."

"Grammy, you should have told me that earlier."

She just grinned and patted his back. "I'm so happy you're home, baby. I'm just so happy, Theory."

He was too. As he started eating again and could feel eyes on him, he looked up and saw Celina was licking her lips, eyeing him hard. She was one of them kind. She was wasting her time. He wasn't interested even a little bit. He didn't like chicks that resembled Fraggle Rock rejects. There was nothing sexy about that. He for sure wanted nothing to do with her and her Rainbow CHOT coalition. Girl, bye!

Chapter 3

irtuous got out of the passenger's side of the
Chevrolet Equinox and immediately opened the
back door to get Tory and Maddison out. Jason
was standing by the hatchback playing with his
iPhone. He didn't even ask about what had happened to
Addison. It was like she just didn't exist, but then again, Greg
had told them that she had left the family and that Virtuous
was *Mom* now. That was weird, but nobody argued with Greg.
Thankfully, they just continued calling her Vivi, except for
Tory and Greg called her Virtue.

Greg came around to her side of the SUV with Tory's
stroller and Virtuous sat her down and locked her in. Then
Greg picked up Maddison. The family crossed the street,
headed toward the Tommy Hilfiger Outlet Store first. Greg
wasn't wealthy, but his family was comfortable. His parents
owned a working organic farm that was doing extremely well.
His oldest brother, Norman, helped run it while Greg had
followed in the footsteps of his maternal uncle and gone into
law enforcement. Not only was he the resource officer at her
high school, but he was also over the Police Explorer Program

at the school, which was how he kept eyes on her pretty much twenty-four-seven.

"Virtue, get the girls two outfits a piece, and you can get something too, but let me see it on you before you try to buy it," he warned.

Virtuous nodded and started in the children's section first while Greg and Jason looked over in the men's section. She liked to dress Tory in dresses and leggings and quickly found her two outfits. She told Greg that getting Tory's clothes at Walmart was just fine because she was going to poop and throw up on them anyway, but he liked them to have name brands sometimes. Virtuous didn't care about it. She was never a materialistic person. People put too much stock in tangible items and not enough in God.

Once the girls were squared away, she looked for something for herself. She really liked the distressed jeans, but she wasn't sure if Greg would approve. He was really controlling like that and had been since she'd come into his care. He'd even done the same to Addison. It was sad that a grown woman couldn't choose her own clothes.

"No," the deep tenor whispered in her ear.

Without questioning why, Virtuous put them back. A second later, the saleswoman came over and asked if they needed help, but Greg sent her away.

"Well, maybe you should pick it out. You know my size, and I'm not good at shopping for myself as I am for the girls," she submitted. That was what he liked anyway. It was sad, but she fed into his male chauvinistic ways.

"Yeah, I don't want you showing those horny high school boys my body. You can get those skinny jeans right there and those boyfriend jeans right there too but let me see them on you. I almost forgot, you need another dress for church too."

"I can get one at like Ross or Marshall's. They're usually cheaper."

"Nah, let's just get it from here."

Virtuous nodded, but that was stupid because she could get two or possibly, three brand name dresses for the cost of one dress in the store. But if he wanted to flex his finances, who was she to argue? After modeling clothes for Greg, he chose what he wanted her to wear and then they were off to the shoe store. They had more time to kill.

The plan was to eat at Outback Steakhouse and then to go the Big E, which was a movie theater that also had a game section for children. Maddison and Jason's overgrown butts were excited about going. It was rare to have a Friday off, so she knew Greg wanted to make a big deal out of it. She was sure they would end up at his family farm because he needed to tell his parents about Addison.

Once they got in the shoe store, Maddison had to pee. She was doing the universal dance. "Daddy, she's got to use the restroom, can I take her?" Virtuous queried.

"Yeah, we'll wait on you here."

Virtuous nodded and took Maddison by the hand and the pair power walked to the restroom. In her rush, she bumped into a guy, a *big* guy. He was with another man and she quickly excused herself and apologized.

"It's cool lil'ma." His silky voice vibrated. It sounded as smooth as butter and caused her to look back. Yes, Lawd, she drunk in him like she was in a drought and he was Fiji water. She was slurping and salivating. Virtuous looked him up and down and he simply smiled knowingly. She ought to have been ashamed of herself, but she couldn't find shame if she'd had directions.

"You like what you see?" he taunted, his succulent pink lips glistened from him licking them, sending impure thoughts through her mind.

Virtuous couldn't take her eyes off him. She did like what she saw, and it felt both right and wrong. He was an extremely attractive young man. He was a tall with a beautiful hue of brown and he was built, but not overly so, just enough to let you know he took care of his body. His skin was unscarred and even toned, not even a tattoo was visible. He had eyelashes and eyebrows that any model, male or female, would be envious of, but there was something about him that wasn't dangerous but *different*. It was his *eyes*. They were bright and brilliant, but they had also seen pain just like her. They were kindred spirits in that way. Virtuous shivered at the instant connection she felt towards a man who was a total stranger to her, and yet he seemed like a longtime acquaintance. She could feel herself floating.

"Vivi, I gotta pee!" Maddison blurted out, bringing Virtuous back to the present and pulling her out of the hypnotic haze she was under. That had never happened before. She was completely bewitched.

Shaking her head, she picked Maddison up and ran her through the food court and into the bathroom. While Maddison used the bathroom, Virtuous tried to gather her thoughts. Who was he and why had he impacted her so? It was like his gaze had held her body prisoner and the scary part was that she wanted to feel that feeling again. That was crazy because she didn't react to men like that. If anything, she did her best to be invisible, especially with a man of his size and stature all because of how Greg treated her. Yet, Greg was the furthest person from her mind when she'd crossed paths with Mr. Handsome. She mentally chastised herself before cleaning Maddison and helping her wash her hands. Whatever had happened could not and would not occur again. As far as she could see, her body was on loan to Greg for the foreseeable future, even though she wished it to be untrue. If it weren't for Maddison and Tory, she would have run away already.

As they exited the restroom, Virtuous did her best to pay attention to her surroundings. She didn't see Mr. Handsome or his friend as she exited the food court and headed back to the shoe store. Letting out a sigh of relief, her body instantly tensed when she heard his voice.

"Looking for me?" that same hypnotic voice questioned.

It melted Virtuous instantly. She closed her eyes as he spoke to quiet the wild thumping of her heart. Somehow, she found the strength to fight the fog. Still, she was puzzled at how he had that type of effect on her. However, he didn't seem to be losing interest and instead, sought a conversation with her. It was a little awkward because she wasn't used to men speaking to her, due to fear of Greg's reaction. Either he would hang around her signaling to other men that she was off limits or he would just threaten her. Honestly, she was in a constant state of panic. Yet she was willing to sacrifice all for two seconds of this man's attention.

"What's your name, beautiful?" he asked with his chestnut eyes danced flirtatiously with interest. Had she been confident like her friend, Tamari, she would have come back with a classy response, but she lacked that ability. Unable to find her voice to respond to his simple question, her sister decided to do it for her. "I'm Maddison and she's Vivi."

Virtuous looked down at her sister who was smiling at the handsome man in front of them who was probably around nineteen. Her little sister had more game than she did. Virtuous couldn't believe how open and friendly her sister was with a stranger. Maddison usually didn't do strangers. She kept her distance, yet she seemed to like this guy. "Hush, Maddison. We don't talk to strangers," she fussed.

"Sorry," she pouted.

Then Mr. Handsome leaned down and got right on Maddison's level. "Hello, Maddison, I'm Theory. Now, we're not strangers are we Cutie."

"Nice to meet you, Theery," Maddison replied, unable to correctly pronounce his name, which made Virtuous smile despite herself. This guy was smooth and charming. His million-dollar smile helped too. He had perfectly aligned white teeth and a friendly demeanor that would disarm any woman.

"Same to you, sweetheart," he replied with a wink as he stood up straight, making Virtuous stretch her neck to see him.

"Well, we should be going," Virtuous quipped. She was feeling nervousness and something else in the pit of her stomach. It wasn't hunger, at least not for food. If life were different, if she weren't terrified of Greg, she would have really liked to get to know Theory, but as it stood, that wasn't an option. They'd been gone long enough, and Greg or Jason could pop up on her at any time. She didn't want that trouble.

"Mmm, you shole are mean. I thought Southern people were friendly."

"I'm sorry, Theory, but we don't have time to socialize. It was nice to meet you and have a great day. I'm really not trying to be rude."

"Hold up, Vivi, let me get your number."

She froze, not sure what to say, but finally found her voice. "I don't have my phone. I left it with my family," she answered honestly.

Theory frowned and looked a little lost, and she replayed what she said in her head and it didn't make sense. She was such an idiot. So, he just asked her the same question differently. "Okay, give me your number and I'll call you."

That couldn't happen because Greg checked her phone. "Just give me yours and I'll remember it. I have a photographic memory."

He chuckled. "You tryna play me? Technically, you already played me. I outta just take my L and move on," he mumbled the latter.

Virtuous really didn't have time for this. "No, I'm not playing you technically or otherwise. I'm just not used to meeting guys. I'm sorry. I'll catch up with you another time," she managed to say before taking Maddison in her arms and jetting away. She could hear Theory chuckling, but she didn't care. If Greg caught them talking, she would have a sore behind. He didn't play about that. He was jealous, possessive, and controlling and she didn't want to piss him off. Greg was in a good mood and Virtuous wanted him to stay that way.

"Maddison, don't tell Daddy about the new friend we made or we'll both be in trouble."

"Okay, Vivi, I won't tell."

When they arrived back in the store, Greg had already bought shoes and was ready to go eat.

"What took you all so long?"

"There was a line. You know how the women's restroom is."

Greg nodded and they all followed him out of the store and strolled toward Outback. As soon as they got settled, Virtuous saw Theory with two guys. She knew one was with him before because she had seen him when they'd collided, but not the other guy. He was slender with dark skin. He was in the beginning stages of growing dreads. She quickly dropped her gaze when she felt Greg's glare on her.

"Did you see someone you know?" he asked, looking behind him.

"No, I just thought they were students from my school," Virtuous lied. She hoped God would forgive her for telling so many lies back to back, but the truth would have her looking like Addison. She just didn't want to get beat up.

"Oh, okay. What do you want to eat?"

There was no reason to ask her that when he was going to tell her what she was eating anyway. He still liked to play the stupid game. "I don't know. What do you think I should get?" He laughed, his dark blue eyes glowing with humor. He loved being in control. No matter how small or large, if he was controlling it, he was happy.

He truly wasn't an unattractive man. In fact, he was handsome for forty. He looked about a decade younger because he kept himself in good shape, ate well, and drank like a gallon of water a day. He was six feet even, had dirty blonde hair that he kept in a military cut, and a body that most men dreamed they had. Women were always checking him out, but he pretended like he didn't notice, although he ate up the attention like a starving man. It wasn't that she cared because she wanted him to find someone else, so he would stop sleeping with her.

Shaking his head, Greg reached out and patted her hand. "I swear if I wasn't with you, you'd be so lost, Virtue. We'll get a blooming onion and you'll get that pasta you like. Maddison will get the chicken strip kid's meal. Jason, you can get what you want, and I'm getting a steak."

Virtuous just nodded as he told all of that to the waitress when she arrived. Greg decided she could eat the pasta dish and that was just fine with her. He would pay for it, so she wasn't going to voice an opinion. It wasn't like he cared or respected whatever she thought or felt.

As they were settling in and eating the bread the waitress had brought to them, Virtuous looked up and caught Theory's crystallized sorrel eyes and she quickly dropped her head. She was really playing with fire, knowing how unstable Greg's temper could be. Yet, Theory was magnetic. Even the boys at her school and church didn't hold her attention like Theory. If she wasn't careful, he'd be the death of her.

"Daddy, after this can we play at the arcade?" Jason asked.

Yup, even Jason called Greg Daddy. Jason was nineteen and in college and he had a hero worship of Greg. Since he was his only father figure, Virtuous understood, but she prayed that Jason would never become his adoptive father.

"Yeah, you can play a few games. I think that ought to be fun for you." Then the two started chatting about sports and Virtuous tuned them out as she tended to Tory who was hungry. She was at that stage where she didn't need a bottle and could eat table food. She usually made Tory's baby food. She was so attentive to what she was doing that she didn't notice Maddison attempting to get her attention.

"Hey, Maddison and Vivi," Theory greeted them like they were old friends.

Just like that, the conversation at the table ceased. Virtuous broke out in a cold sweat and implored God that Theory wouldn't ask for her number while she was with Greg and Jason.

"Hey," Maddison replied sweetly, grinning all over herself.

"I'm sorry, but who are you?" Greg quizzed. His dark blonde eyebrows knitted as his eyes pranced from Maddison to Virtuous and then to Theory.

Fear grasped Virtuous, causing her to go mute. All she could do was observe in silence.

"No need to apologize. I'm Theo. I'm friends with your daughters. I just wanted to say hello. Excuse me for interrupting you all's meal. I'll talk to you later, Vivi."

"Bye," Maddison called out.

"Bye, cutie."

Before he was gone good, Greg turned his eyes on Virtuous. "Who is he, Virtue?" He seethed.

Virtuous managed find her voice. "I don't know. I just bumped into him."

He shook his head. "He spoke as if you two were acquainted and I don't like it. You better not be lying to me," he fumed, his entire demeanor had changed, and she didn't want him to beat on her like he did Addison.

"I'm not. The God honest, truth is I bumped him," she defended with a distressed face and she was thankful when the fire died in his eyes. She mentally prayed to God for saving her from that one.

"Virtue, you've got to be careful, honey. I know you're friendly and all, but everyone isn't your friend. That guy looks like a thug. Did he give you a hard time? If he did, I can handle it now."

"No, Daddy, he was nice," Maddison assured.

Greg nodded, but Virtuous knew he didn't like the situation. At least she would never see Theory again, so it didn't matter.

A &Ω

Theory, Archie, and their buddy, Shalamar, were hanging out for the day. Even though it was an in-service school day, Val was at school watching his game films with his coaches. Dude was dedicated, and Theory respected that. They had done a little shopping because Theory honestly didn't need a thing. His family had really come through for him, which still had him in shock. He was just chilling this weekend because next week he was hitting the pavement to look for a job and get himself in somebody's college. He owed that much to Grammy.

Theory and the guys entered Outback Steakhouse, he was still thinking about his strange encounter with Vivi. She looked familiar, but he couldn't place her. It was weird and her reaction to him was as well. He was a good-looking dude, and that wasn't being arrogant or presumptuous. It was just God's truth. He had been up here for an hour and had a massive amount of numbers and he wasn't even checking for chicks. He wasn't sure if it was a man drought or if chicks were just that thirsty. At any rate, the only woman on his mind was Vivi, who hadn't giving him her number. He would've called her. There was something about her that felt kindred.

Anyway, they were taken to a table right away, and there she was. He didn't know why this chick was in his head, but she was. He thought she was just a light-skinned girl but seeing her surrounded by white people made him think she was biracial, which would explain her reaction to him. The girl probably didn't know any black people. She was most likely raised by the white side of her family, but she had the body of a sistah for real. He wondered where her mother was.

"Vicious, who are you eyeing that hard?" Shalamar asked.

"Didn't I tell you to call me Theo or Theory? I'm letting that Vicious persona go. I'm not that dude no more. Anyhow, it's lil'ma right there." Shalamar looked where his head nodded.

"I didn't think AKA sorority-looking girls were your thing. You know I like my girls thick and dark chocolate, but whatever gives you the feels. How old is she? Is that her baby? Dang, girls be eight and having babies and the grandmas be seventeen and the great-grandmas be twenty-nine. Believe me, bruh. You don't want a chick with a kid. That means she got a baby daddy and that equals problems!"

Theory and Archie burst into laughter, causing those close to them to look at them, but they didn't care.

"Sha, you's a fool, man. That don't even add up. You know they got to have a monthly before they can have a baby. Eight-year-old girls ain't going through puberty."

"Dude, for real, though, per research black girls go through puberty earlier than other races. I learned that in my social work class."

"Oh, I forgot you're in your junior year of college. He might be right," Archie agreed.

"But *eight*? Man, that's messed up. I don't think that's her baby. I think they're her sisters. That built dude must be her daddy and beside him, I think that's her brother."

"Aye, ain't she mixed, though? I mean she can pass, but that 3C curl pattern is a dead giveaway even if it's honey blonde. The rest of them look white to me. Somebody's momma went dipping in the black lake. As Maury would say, *"You are not the father!"*

Archie dropped his bread and fell over laughing. "Why are you so stupid, Sha? How you know about curl patterns? Sometimes you trouble me."

Ignoring Archie, Theory replied, "Man, I don't know all of that. She could be adopted or even the babysitter. I didn't get that far when I met her. She was acting scary."

"Well, whatever she is, she's cute, but she ain't got nothing on the girls we going to see at the club tonight. We should hit up Charlotte, but I'm scared Grammy going to come out pistol popping if I bring you home too late or take you across state lines. You know she's on that Madea tip," Archie goaded.

"Pistol popping?" Theory asked, laughing. "You know Grammy is a woman of God. She ain't gonna shoot you. Besides, Grammy's cool. She's just glad I'm home, but I think I want to stay close to home. Sparkle City will have to do for tonight."

The fellas were conversing, but Theory felt eyes on him, so he looked up and saw Vivi checking for him. Then she dropped her head, causing him to become curious. This girl was for real interested in him. He wondered what Vivi was short for. Was it Victoria, Vivian, or Venita? He was going check her out. He told his boys he was heading to the restroom.

Theory purposely sauntered by Vivi's table and Maddison caught his eye, so he had to speak. She was a cute little girl.

She had shoulder-length blonde hair and big blue eyes. She was attempting to get Vivi's attention, but she was busy feeding her little sister and Theory was trying to figure out where the mother was. Then he wondered if Vivi was the babysitter and not the daughter.

"Hey, Maddison and Vivi," he greeted them, apparently startling Vivi as Maddison spoke. Then the guy that was with them gave him a serious mean mug after they had a little introductory conversation. He was sure that old dude was her daddy because he had that don't-mess-with-my-daughter look, which cracked Theory up. He said goodbye and headed to the restroom.

Theory strolled the same way he had come after using the restroom. He was being petty because he'd heard the daddy call him a thug, and it was funny to him how red the dude had turned. He was big mad and that was entertaining. By the time he strolled by them, they were praying over their food. That made him like Vivi a little more. She had manners, she cared about what her father thought so she was more than likely a good girl, and she took care of her siblings. Plus, she was pretty.

She was a natural beauty. She wore no makeup, no false lashes, or rocked an outrageous hairstyle. Her nails were even natural. He liked real women. Most women were beautiful in their natural state and all of that extra they put on like they were decorating a Christmas tree took away from their natural beauty. That was *his* opinion. Some dudes loved all that. That was what had really caught his eye about Vivi. She didn't need decorations because she was enough just the way she was.

Vivi had her hair pulled up in a bun. He assumed it was all hers. She was slim thick, probably no more than a size eight. Her skin shimmered and she had some pretty hazel eyes that kind of reminded him of Val's. She wasn't that tall, though. She was probably five-six or five-seven, but she was an eye catcher. Theory wanted her number, so hopefully, she lived close. He got an idea. He was going to ask the waitress to give her his number on the low. He took a picture of her while she was praying. He would find out her identity if she didn't call him. Feeling a bit perv-ish, he padded back to his table where his boys were working on their second helping of bread. He wasn't big on bread, so he didn't care that they weren't saving him any.

"Man, what'd you say to ole girl, because her pops was going in on her."

"I just spoke to her. I guess he didn't like it, but whatever. Where's my salad at?"

"It's coming, withcha impatient self. See, here comes our waitress now."

Theory looked back and Vivi was looking at him again. He smiled and winked at her before turning his attention back to his food. That girl was going to get him in trouble. Her daddy looked like one of them shotgun carrying, camo-wearing, eat-road-kill kind of fools. He didn't need those problems, yet he wanted the man's daughter.

Theory ate the remainder of his meal and when the time came, he put his plan into motion. He watched with hawk eyes when the waitress did as he'd asked. The father had gone to the restroom, but her brother was still there. He was deeply engaged in a game on his phone. Surprisingly, Vivi took his number, but she had a perplex look on her face, wondering why the paper had been given to her. Then the waitress nodded his way and he and Vivi's eyes caught. He winked at her and she offered him a small smile. She folded the paper and put it into her bra, which he got a kick out of and chuckled. Then he mouthed to her to call him, just as the father was coming back.

Chapter 4

On their way back from Gaffney, the family stopped by Greg's parents' home, which was also a working organic farm and store. Greg wanted to let his parents know about what had happened between him and Addy. However, Virtuous' head had been in the clouds since getting Theory's number. It was burning a hole in her bra, but she couldn't chance removing it until she got home. Instead, she turned her attention to Mamaw LeAnn. She was a petite little thing with bleached blonde hair to hide her gray. She had crystal blue eyes, which both her sons had inherited.

"She left you and the children?" Mamaw queried. Her eyebrows nearly reached her hairline, which happened whenever she got excited.

Virtuous sat quietly on the couch while Greg discussed with his parents and brother about Addison leaving the family. Honestly, he hadn't given her much of a choice, but Virtuous didn't speak on that. Truth be told, she was too busy contemplating calling Theory. But what would she say? He was so dapper, and she couldn't believe he had risked Greg's ire for her. Then again, he didn't know her secrets nor was he aware of the depravity of the man she called Daddy.

"Yes. I expected it after I found out about her affair with a co-worker. We're getting a divorce and I'm keeping the kids. I don't want her influencing them. It has gone too far now. She's really gone off on her addiction and won't go to rehab, so what else can I do? I had to claw her off Virtue," Greg replied with a hint of desperation in his tone.

Virtuous couldn't believe the Oscar-award-winning performance he was giving off. He even he had her believing his farce of a story. Greg was the problem. Addison wouldn't have gone off the deep end if he hadn't turned into a sicko, raping his own daughter. That was the huge piece of information that Mamaw LeAnn and Papaw Neman didn't have. There were so many times she wanted to confide in them, but they would never believe her word over their own son.

"My Lord, sweetheart, you're right. You can't force her to get help, but the children don't need to be around that at all. I'll help you with Maddison and Tory. I know it has to be hard."

"Thanks, Mom. Virtue is doing a good job at being a mom, but I need all the help I can get."

"Of course, honey. Vivi, how're you dealing with things? I'm so sorry she assaulted you. I mean I just can't understand what has happened to Addison." She shook her head in dismay before going typical granny. "Oh, baby, are you okay?" LeAnn fussed, walking over and embracing Virtuous with the warmth that only a grandmother could offer.

That was what Virtuous didn't want to lose. She wished that Greg would just treat her as his daughter and nothing more like his family treated her.

"I'm fine. I know it was just the drugs. She didn't mean it."

"I don't like it," Papaw quipped. "Son, you should've had her arrested for attacking that child. Vivi's had enough hardship and she didn't deserve that. Did you take her to the hospital?"

"Papaw, it wasn't that severe. Daddy got her off me quickly."

"It should have never happened," Norman fumed, shaking his head. "I told you about her. She's trailer trash. Vivi's the sweetest child I've ever met. There was no reason to attack her, but that's what trash does."

"Norman, don't say such in front of Vivi. That's still her mother."

"I can go. I should check on my sisters anyway," Virtuous offered.

"Go ahead, sweetheart," Greg urged.

A &Ω

After talking to his family, they agreed divorce was the answer. Greg piled his family in the SUV and headed home. He knew that Virtuous liked to go over Maddison's Sunday School lesson, so he wanted to get home, so she could get prepared. Since his mom cooked, Virtue didn't have to. She wanted to get ahead in a project she had due in one of her advanced placement classes.

When they arrived home, Jason went upstairs to play his gaming system, Tory was sleeping so he took her upstairs and Virtue and Maddison went to Greg's office to do their work. After putting Tory down, he shuffled into his bedroom and showered. Once he was done, he laid on the bed and turned on the television. He was watching a Criminal Minds rerun when his cellphone started ringing.

"Yes?"

"Greg, it's me, Addison. I tried to get some money out of my account, but it's empty. I know you're mad at me, but I need some money until my next payday."

"Nope. Ask your little boyfriend for the money or your family. What I make is for me and my children. You need to just say no to drugs, and you might have something."

"Greg, you can't be serious. Okay, I admit I was wrong to put hands on Virtuous. She's not the problem. If you just help me get into rehab, then we can be a family again. I'm begging, baby. Please forgive me."

Before he could reply he heard a male voice in the background. He presumed it was her new man, so he hung up and then blocked her number. He went back to watching television and must have dozed off because when he woke up again it was dark outside, but Virtue wasn't in his bed. That was soon to be rectified.

He got up and went in search of her. He stopped first by the girls' bedroom, but no Virtuous. The girls were asleep, so he jogged downstairs and found Virtuous asleep on the couch holding her physics textbook. He smiled. His baby was all about her books. She was intelligent, loyal, sweet, submissive, and crazy about her family. His heart fluttered a little as he observed her lips part. She was the sweetest sin.

He smiled and lifted her in his arms and brought her back to the bedroom. Once he placed her in bed, he kissed her, trying to wake her up. She mumbled something inaudible. "Wake up, Virtue," he coaxed, but she seemed to be in a deep slumber, so he didn't bother her. Besides, sometimes he just liked watching her sleep. He'd get her later. Greg pulled her body into his, breathing in her scent of lavender mixed with vanilla. Then he slowly dozed off, his breathing falling in sync with hers.

A &Ω

The boys had persuaded Theory to hit up Anderson to hang out. They were headed to a house party instead of the club, so Val was riding with them. Theory hadn't been to the area since juvie, but it didn't look like much had changed. Once they arrived at Trek's house they were quickly greeted by familiar faces. Theory made sure to tell Val to stay close. He didn't want anything popping off around Val. He had too many great opportunities and no one was taking that from him. The only reason Grammy had allowed Val to come was because they'd promised to keep him safe.

They did a walk-through around the party and then settled down in the backyard just chilling and chopping it up. Theory kept his eyes open because he knew Nocturnal, who thought of himself as the man in the streets, might roll up and he really wasn't in the mood. Theory was done with that thug life. He hadn't been initiated into Noc's crew because he had gotten locked up before it happened, and he was glad about it. That had been a blessing in disguise. At his age, he couldn't see himself hanging on a corner reppin' a sect. It just lost its appeal after he did his time.

"Theo, look there goes your cousin, Maisha, and that chick, Nora Jean."

"Ain't she too uppity for a house party? I thought she'd be down in Atlanta in one of them upscale clubs with celebrities, but she out here in the country. What kind of backwoods name is Nora Jean anyway? It sounds like a country singer's stage name." Theory chuckled. "I mean she ain't going to find a suga daddy up in here."

"Right! I can't stand a Save-A-Lot chick thinking she's a Whole Foods Market. That's just embarrassing. We both know all she got in her wallet is a Rush Card, EBT card, and a Walmart gift card so she can get three cents off when she gets unleaded gas for her 2006 Nissan Versa. She needs to stop fronting, ole Section 8 strumpet. Out here acting like she got Benjamins when all she got is Monopoly money. She's faking and finessing dudes left and right."

"You're stupid, Archie. I swear, man. Where you come up with that mess? Man, I just died for three seconds. I can't with you, bruh. Then you got Val tripping just like you!" Theory laughed out and Val was hunched over killing himself laughing. Archie was a fool.

"I dunno. It just be coming to me. I gotta be creative now. I can't say whore, hoe, or ho no more. Grammy hit cha boy up with that Dial Gold antibacterial soap for a good ten minutes. I'm talkin' 'bout she scrubbed my mouth out. My tongue newborn baby clean; I'll never catch the flu. Ya heard me?" he asked, but his eyes caught something, and his attention shifted again. "Oh shoot, look at thick and sexy, bruh! I gotta say hello to that."

Theory guffawed so hard at Archie's admission. That sounded like Grammy. "Do you, Archie. I'm just chillin'."

"Theo, I'ma go holla at Trek," Val told him who had been laughing as well.

"Go 'head." Theory watched Val leave and then turned his attention back to Arch who dapped with that Denzel Washington swagger over to the girl he was eyeing. Theory was killing himself laughing. Archie swore he was the man.

"What's so funny, sexy?"

Theory turned to the voice and nearly swallowed his tongue and teeth. He hadn't seen *this* female since he'd been arrested. Her name was Staci and she had done him dead wrong. The crew he called himself unofficially rolling with, Nocturnal and them, were fake friends. As soon as he got locked up, Staci was on to the next one. The last he had heard Staci was with Nocturnal, so he could have her.

Lord, forgive him, but time hadn't been good to her. She had that face beat to death and still looked like somebody's ninety-year-old, wrinkly grandma. She had more lines than a piece of college-rule notebook paper like her face was a carbon copy of the African plains during the dry season. Yeah, it was that deeply cracked. Ain't nothing Shea Moisture, Black Opal or Iman Cosmetics could do to fix that or even organic coconut oil. Staci needed to touch the hem of Jesus' garment to heal that face. As if that wasn't bad enough, her stomach was fighting the fabric of the dress she was wearing. Whoever her homegirls were, they ought to have been shot for allowing her to leave the house like that. On the real, she had no friends if she strutted in public like this here. He just shook his head. He was better dressed in his juvie uniform.

It would have been better if she had just ignored him instead of allowing him to see her at her worst. By no means was he feenin' for what she was showcasing. Theory assumed Staci had given birth to like two or three babies and her body had just refused to bounce back. She was just twenty-three, but she was aging in dog years. It was a shame, but better Nocturnal than him.

Theory turned his head and nodded to the music like Staci wasn't standing there, which should have indicated that he wasn't pressed for her or interested in having a conversation. But for some reason, she was a little slow to comprehend that. It was just a second later before he heard her annoying voice again.

"Theory, it's me, *Staci*," she quipped like that was supposed to mean something to him. Theory looked at her hand on his forearm and thumped it off. He was funny about strangers putting their hands on him. Even before he got locked up, he didn't like people touching him. He blamed that on his childhood.

"Don't call me Theory. The name is Vicious to you. That's number one. Second, keep your hands to yourself. I get offended when people touch me without my permission. Lastly, I was trying to be nice and ignore you to save you this humiliation, but you seem to want your feelings hurt. So, bounce. I don't know you and you don't know me. Take your broke-down Trina wannabe self out my face cause you ain't da baddest, you da saddest. Exit out my line of sight right now and don't come back, ever!" There was no residual hurt from her betrayal. Nah, Theory was just telling what he knew, which was the truth.

The look on Staci's face was priceless, but he didn't care. What she looked like dipping on him for Nocturnal and now that Theory was a free man and looking better than ever, she was up in his face? *These females are straight trifling out here.* No wonder Archie called them Section 8 strumpets. That was a foul move.

Theory held her gaze, giving her the cruelest mean mug, he could muster and didn't even blink. An array of emotion fled her face, but he was unbothered. Finally, she got it and stepped away. *Good.* A few minutes later, Archie came back with the woman he was checking earlier and two of her friends. Yeah, this was going to be an early night. He was seriously regretting not getting Vivi's phone number now. He needed something new because seeing his ex-girlfriend had really screwed up his night.

Chapter 5

Staci stood in the kitchen making breakfast for her son and daughter, but her mind was in another place. She knew that Vicious would be getting out this year, so when she heard about Trek's house party and that Vicious might be coming through, she got cute and sought him out. He was still fine, finer, but that attitude was atrocious. She had never expected him to shade her to the left like he had. It hurt. Yeah, she should have been a better girlfriend, but she was seventeen at the time. She was older than Vicious by two years, but he had swagger about him that made up for his youth. He was a street kid, however. He wasn't corner-boy material, but he was known on the streets for his hands. That man could fight. He should've been a boxer or an MMA fighter. It shocked the heck out of her that he had caught a robbery charge. She had thought if he ever got locked up it would be an assault charge.

"Aye, whatchu cooking, Staci?" Noc's deep voice vibrated through the kitchen. With so much bass, one would expect him to be over six feet tall, but he was only five-feet-ten and weighed about one hundred sixty. Staci licked her lips when he entered the kitchen. His shirt was off, tattoos showing with nothing but pajama bottoms. He had a creamy peanut butter complexion with long neat dreads. He had that thug appeal. Nothing about him said suit and tie. That just wasn't his style, but he conducted himself in a way that was just mesmerizing.

"Hey, Daddy!" the children enthusiastically greeted their father.

"Hey, Runt 1 and Runt 2," Nocturnal teased them, kissing the tops of their heads.

Staci smiled, but she and Nocturnal had been having relationship issues as of late. However, he for sure loved the kids and they loved him. For the leader of a crew, he was down to earth and could be sweet, but there was always that other side that lingered. Staci understood it. To his credit, he was shifting the guys from drugs to gambling, clubs, and trying to get an underground fighting ring. She appreciated him changing his focus because of his family. Staci wasn't tripping on that, but she wanted more of a commitment from him. They had been through a lot over the years. Trust issues and infidelity had put a rift between them, but they always came back together and now she wanted more.

Staci just wished he would put an engagement ring on her finger and make her his wife. That would make her feel more secure. She'd been holding him down for nearly six years, had blessed him with two children, and was pregnant with a third one, but he kept telling her he didn't need paper to tell him that he loved his family. But *she* did. Staci didn't want to be like her momma, popping out babies with no ring on her finger and no commitment on paper. She wanted the title of wife and not baby momma. If Vicious hadn't been locked up, he would have married her. His grandmother had raised him right on that.

"Did you hear me, Staci? I asked whatcha cooking. And do something to my daughter's hair. You got her looking like the Bride of Chucky."

Staci rolled her eyes hard at Noc trying to be funny. But she answered his question because she heard the annoyance and impatience in his voice. They didn't need to start a Sunday morning off arguing in front of the kids. "Her hair will be done before we leave. I'm making grits, ham with the bone in, turkey bacon, biscuits, and eggs. I'm frying some for you and scrambling egg whites for your picky kids."

"That's what's up. Don't be complaining about their eating habits when you let'em go to that white church's after-school program. Got my son talking like he from the suburbs. I dunno why they can't go to my momma's house," he complained.

"I love your momma, but she smokes, and Sadie got asthma and you know smoke is one of her triggers. Also, Chauncory don't like how her house smells. It makes his allergies cut up." Staci defended.

Staci heard him suck his teeth, but he didn't say anything. Instead, he took his five-feet-ten self out of the kitchen, flopped on the couch, and turned on the television, drowning out the children's chatter and ignoring her.

Ten minutes later, Staci called everyone to come eat. She was making plates for everyone, but she only had a taste for dry Apple Jacks cereal. She just couldn't do milk with this pregnancy. This child she was carrying was choosey. It would like something one day and she'd be throwing up the same thing the next day.

"Staci, I know you eating more than that. You better feed my seed," Noc fussed.

The last thing she needed to do was eat more. Staci needed to be in a gym doing yoga and Pilates to get her body back. This child she was having now was stealing her glow, beauty, and body. She hated it. Honestly, she didn't want to be pregnant again. At twenty-three, she was already on baby number three. She didn't care what Noc said. She was getting on birth control or her tubes tied. They had enough children.

"I am, but this little one here don't like nothing. Unless you want me to throw up everything, all I can do is dry cereal."

"Well, if you weren't at a house party last night wit ya girls, then maybe my baby wouldn't be making you sick," he snapped.

She rolled her eyes and started eating and watching her kids. Sadie would sometimes put too much in her mouth, trying to eat fast like her daddy and get choked.

"Chauncey, are you going with me to handle some business?" Noc asked his son.

"Daddy, it's Sunday."

"And? What that 'pose to mean?"

"Daddy, you aren't supposed to work on the Sabbath day. That's for rest and worship. I'm going to Sunday school and church with Mommy," his son replied politely.

Staci couldn't help but laugh at her son's reply. He wasn't any kind of gangsta, which was what Noc wanted. She disapproved, which was why she took her children to church Wednesday and Sunday. "Why you call my baby Chauncey when his name is Chauncory?"

"Because I told your uppity, hood self to name the boy something I can say. I don't wanna pronounce all of that. I told you to name him after me, but no, you wanted to be fancy. Chill out, because Chauncey is just a nickname like Nocturnal is mine."

Staci laughed at him. He was so ignorant. "Well, whatever. It's *Shaun-Co-ry*. How is that hard? I wasn't naming my baby Percival Cadell Kershaw Junior."

"Keep making fun of my name," he warned.

Staci left it alone, knowing he was sensitive about his government name. Lawd knew his momma must have been high to name him Percival. She claimed she'd named him after the fictional character Percival who was one of King Arthur's Legendary Knights of the Round Table. She should have at least chosen the name Lancelot. They could've made that work. His sister was named Penelope Guinevere Kershaw. Their mother had done the most with her names.

"Daddy, are you coming to church with us?" Sadie asked as she got up and plopped herself on her father's lap. She was holding her jelly biscuit and making a mess. She was one hundred percent a daddy's girl and Nocturnal ate it up.

"Not this time, baby girl, but I'll get you next week," he told her as he stole a bite off her biscuit, making Staci grin. She reached out and ran her hand down his face.

"Stop, Staci. You see me eating. That's rude."

"Fine! Excuse me," she snapped and got up from the kitchen table.

"Staci, stop with the dramatics and sit back down and feed my seed. You know last time you got dizzy and nearly fainted. If you let that happen again I'ma make you pay for it."

Staci ignored him and went to take a shower. Sometimes, she wished she had waited for Vicious to get out. However, the way Vicious had treated her last night let her know that he was still in his feelings about how she had hopped from one bed to the next, but really, Noc was coming up and coming so strongly and Vicious just wasn't into being a corner boy. Noc wasn't a kingpin or anything like that, but they were comfortable, and he was known in the streets. He was a hood celebrity for real, and she liked that. He was getting a house built since he had knocked her up again, but she wanted more. She missed those sweet things that Vicious used to do for her that Noc never did, though.

Closing her eyes, she let the warm water cascade down her body. Her mind drifted to what could have been. She needed to reach out to Trek and see where Vicious was. She really wanted to apologize to him. She wasn't sure if he would accept it, but she had to try. She wondered how Noc was going to react to Vicious being released.

"Staci, all I know is you better eat before you leave this house or we going to have some problems!" Noc yelled.

A &Ω

Nocturnal buckled his children in their car seats. Then he turned his attention to Staci. She had eaten the dry cereal, yogurt, toast, and had kept it all down. He didn't know why she wanted to start this morning, but she was on that talk back and he was really contemplating slapping some sense into her head. If she wasn't carrying his child, he would have.

"Y'all eating at'cha momma's house or are you coming home to cook?"

"I'ma take the kids to see her, but I'ma cook at home. How long are you going to be gone?"

He gave her that stay-in-your-lane look. "As long as I need to be. Don't try to clock my movements. We know how that worked out before. Enjoy the service and have my kids in the house, fed, and bathed before seven o'clock 'cause they better be in bed by eight."

"Okay, Noc. Bye." She rolled her eyes, but he didn't care because she knew what was up.

"Love you, Daddy!" the children hollered out.

"I love y'all too. Be good at church. If either of yo grannies tells me y'all was cutting up, I'ma whoop y'all."

"We gon' be real good, Daddy," Sadie promised.

"A'ight then. See y'all later." Then he turned to Staci and kissed her. "You better have a different attitude when you get back." She looked at him astonished like she didn't know what he was talking about. Staci started to defend herself, but he shut that down. "What I say?"

She dramatically rolled her eyes. "Okay, Noc. Can we go now? I'on wanna be late."

"Go," he told her and shut the door. He watched them leave in her sleek black Audi Q7 SUV. His kids waved at him until they couldn't see him anymore. Then he went back to the house to chill before he headed out to link up with his boys. As soon as he got settled, his cell was going off.

It was Congo, and believe it or not, that was his real name. His father was from the Democratic Republic of the Congo, but he was murdered before he was born. His momma named him Congo to honor his father. He was a big dude too, nearly two hundred and fifty pounds of solid steel and nearly six-three. "Yo, what up, Con?"

"Bruh, where was you last night? Trek had a house party and it was lit. Guess who out?"

"Who, man? I ain't got time to play Guess Who, so just tell me."

"Ah, I see it's one of them kind of mornings. Vicious got out. He's huge now. I'm shocked your baby mama didn't tell you. She was over there talking to him."

"Oh yeah? She was up in his face," he questioned, his entire face balling up. Let him find out she still had feelings for Vicious and he would make her life miserable.

"It wasn't nothing like that. He wasn't pressed for her or nobody else. He was just chillin' and keeping to himself. Anyway, is ya coming through?"

"In a bit. I'm just relaxing for a minute. So, did you talk to Vicious or what?"

"Nah, he was with Archie and the light bright. Then they left. I asked Trek if he was back in town to stay, but he said that Vicious wasn't moving back to Anderson. He trying to get his life right, going to college and stuff like that. I was like for real, 'cause he just never came across as that type of dude, but I guess having your freedom snatched from you can change your outlook on life. Ya know what I mean?"

Noc nodded, not that Congo could see it, but that was his response. He wasn't sure how he felt about Vicious being back, but it sure rubbed him wrong that his pregnant girl was out and about chatting it up with her ex. That sure didn't feel right and he was going to get all in her for that.

"Congo, let me holla at you later. Lourdes is beeping in."

"Cool," Congo replied and hung up.

"What it is, Lo?"

"Hey, Noc, I was wondering if you were coming through."

Nocturnal sucked his teeth. He had to be careful with Lo. She was opioid addictive, that's how attractive she was. Girl had an hour-glass figure and she dressed that body like it was royalty. She was about five-eight, rocked those box braids, and stayed slayed. Her face had a natural glow and only was enhanced when she wore makeup and she had the cutest septum piercing and a tongue ring. The girl was his dream and his nightmare.

Nocturnal had met her in Atlanta, Georgia when he was expanding his territory. He was slowly building an empire, but he kept it all low-key even from Staci. He had never been a flashy kind of dude. He had come from nothing, so having a lot of material things wasn't big for him. He wanted to make sure his children had everything they needed. He never wanted his kids to be on public assistance of any type so what he was building was for their future.

"Nah, I ain't making a trip to Atlanta," he replied coolly.

"I can make it worth your wild." There was a flirtatious hum to her already seductive voice.

Yes, she could, but it wouldn't be worth it in the long run. He had been there and done that. That's why he called her his nightmare. "Lo, you know I got a whole family. Why you tryna tempt me? I ain't that dude I used to be."

"I like who you *used to be*. C'mon Noc, I miss you," she whined.

"Nope. I'm good. You just keep my ledgers up to date. I gotta go. For real, don't call me unless it's business. My girl insane and I don't need them kinds of problems again and neither do you. You can underestimate Staci and sleep on her if you want, but it's a deadly mistake."

"Okay, boss. Bye."

Nocturnal must have been growing up because six months ago, an offer like that would have had him saying Staci who? But he'd stopped fooling around with Lo when they'd had a pregnancy scare. He was one of those guys who didn't want several women having his babies. Staci was enough of a handful, because she for sure left him when he was with Lo, she didn't know who the woman was, but she knew something was going down. She took his kids and went to her momma's house for nearly a month and he lost his mind. He loved his kids. Shaking the thoughts, he got up and got ready. He needed to drop some money off at his sister's house. Her dude that worked with him was currently locked up and because Penelope was his sister, he had to take care of her and her children.

After getting ready, he hopped into his Dodge Challenger SRT Hellcat and headed out to over to Toxaway. He was going to stop by his sister's house on the way and then he needed to talk to Congo. He was curious about where Vicious' mind was at because boy had hands like a pro, and he would love to get him into underground fighting. He was trying to transition out of drugs and into gambling and fighting. He was in the process of opening a gym and investing in some clubs in Atlanta.

Chapter 6

Virtuous held Tory as they entered LeAnn's house and Maddison was right on her heels holding the end of Virtuous' dress. Once they got inside, the sweet aroma of cooking food hit her hard. She was so happy she didn't have to cook Sunday dinner. She could do it because she learned from LeAnn, but she didn't feel like cooking today. She just wanted to eat, enjoy family, and hope that Greg wouldn't be rude today.

Before she got in the house good, Cate, Norman's wife reached out for Tory. Everybody loved holding Tory because she was a good baby and she was plump. Her little cheeks were often red from all the kisses everyone planted on her, but Tory just ate it up.

"Hey, Auntie," Maddison chimed. Now, she was holding onto Virtuous' leg. It was adorable. Virtuous ran her fingers through Maddison's hair.

"Hey, sweet girl, are going to come watch the Disney Channel with me and Tory?"

"Yes." She grinned and zoomed off, causing both Virtuous and Cate to laugh.

"Vivi, where's your father and Jason?" Cate asked.

"They're coming." Just as she said that the door opened again, revealing Greg and Jason.

"There you two are."

"Hey, Cate," Greg greeted as he reached for Tory.

"Greg, let me hold her for a while. We're going to watch television."

"Okay. Where's Maddison?"

"Waiting on us. C'mon, Jason and tell me how your classes are going," Cate replied, reaching out for Jason who compiled.

Once they left, Greg turned his attention toward Virtuous. He had a knowing smile on his face that made her entire body shudder. He had been well mannered as he usually was in church, but that could only last so long. So much for her hoping he wouldn't act inappropriately.

"Mom, Virtue and I are going horseback riding we'll be back within the hour!" he shouted through the house.

Before answering him, LeAnn walked out of the kitchen and into the walkway where Virtuous was giving Greg a bewildered look. He knew that she feared horses after she'd fallen off and wanted nothing to do with them. She didn't mind the other animals on the farm, but she drew the line at riding horses.

"Gregory, honey, do you think that best? She's been deathly afraid since the accident."

"Please don't make me ride it. I'm terrified of them." she pleaded.

"Well, the only way to get over a fear is to face it," he told her before turning to his mother. "Mom, she won't ride alone, I'm letting her ride with me. We'll be back soon. Watch Maddison. She'll eat all those Tootsie Rolls that Ms. Harlow gave her."

"I got it, Greg. You both enjoy. Take Tudor. He's the gentlest horse we have."

Greg nodded and reached out for Virtuous' hand, prompting her to take his, and then the pair exited the door together.

Virtuous didn't say much. Her mind was going crazy at the idea of riding a horse. "Daddy, can't I just watch you? I really don't want to ride the horse, not even Tudor," she complained.

He gripped her hand tighter and pulled her body closer to him, causing her to nearly trip, but his strong arms enwrapped her. "You're riding so stop the whining. We need to talk, and I couldn't talk to you in the house. Calm down, okay? I just want some us time," he cooed and then continued to the horse stalls.

Once they arrived, he got the horse ready and got atop of him first and then reached out to help Virtuous get on. "I want you in front of me." his deep tenor pierced the quietude, and she quickly did as he'd requested.

As soon as she settled on the horse that wasn't Tudor, but Hershey Knight, she exhaled a deep breath, and Greg pulled her into his chest and gently kissed her exposed neck. "Calm down, baby. I'm not going to let you fall. You know I love you too much to allow anything to happen to you. Do you trust me?"

She nodded yes out of habit. Honestly, there were certain situations she trusted him with, like paying the bills, providing for his family, being a good cop, but not her body or heart. She knew she was his possession and not in a good way.

"I asked you a question, darling. Therefore, I require an answer that isn't nonverbal," he grilled.

"Yes, Daddy, I trust you."

"Good girl." Then he gave Hershey Knight a command and they started trotting at a slow but constant pace that she tried to be comfortable with. For her, this was torture because she had been thrown off a horse a few years ago that left her with an ugly scar above her right hip.

As the ride continued, Virtuous eased up a little and Greg told her to take the reins and he firmly planted his arms on her. From the outside looking in one might assume it was to secure her, to protect her, but she knew it was his possessiveness and his need to remind her who was in charge.

"Virtue, what happened Friday, between you and that thug can't happen again. Do you understand?" His large hand gripped her thighs as she spoke.

"Yes. I understand."

"You ever make me look like a fool again, having some unsuspecting thug approaching us talking to you or my daughters and I'll show you who you belong to and make you regret it. I've never had to be rough with you, but I can, and I will," his steely voice assaulted her ears. She knew exactly what he was saying, and she wasn't dumb enough to cross him.

"Yes, Daddy," she replied robotically. Greg was extremely conceited and never seemed to pick up on the fact that she only said what he wanted to hear. If he knew the thoughts that really were in her head, he would beat her like he'd done Addison.

She could feel rather than see his satisfactory grin as she submitted to his dominance, but needing to change the tension and conversation, she asked, "Daddy, did you contact the school and aftercare, so Addison won't be able to pick up Tory or Maddison?"

"Yes, and I got an order of protection for me and you kids. I meant to tell you that. It pays to have friends in all walks of life. Also, this week I'm seeing the divorce attorney. I want this mess of a marriage over so that you and I can be free and clear, baby."

She did her best not to react negatively, but she really hated the pet names and being the replacement mommy and wife. She had to find a way to escape the madness. He mistook her quietness for concern. "Hey, you and I are going to be together soon. You'll be my wife like it should be."

Virtuous scowled furiously, but since he was sitting behind her, he couldn't see her face. She had to tread lightly, but she would never give him the chance to marry her. She'd take the girls and run far away. "Daddy, I want to go to college."

"I know and I want you to attend college. There are some good four-year schools here."

"Actually, I was thinking about going out of state." She felt him stiffen and she closed her eyes, praying an argument wouldn't ensue and she wouldn't taste the back of his hand.

"You were thinking? Mmkay, stop the horse let's get off here." he snapped gruffly.

Virtuous did as she'd been told even though fear coursed through her marrow. He got down first, with his aviator sunglasses on so she couldn't read his expression. He assisted her off the horse and led her to the American sycamore tree.

"I thought it was agreed you'd attend college in state," he voiced, sky blue eyes darkening into storm-cloud gray. He pursed his thin lips, making them appear whiter than his body. He was ticked.

Virtuous felt her mouth go dry. Maybe this hadn't been the best time to bring up the news. "I just want to keep my options open. I want to live someplace other than Boiling Springs, South Carolina. I mean honestly, how long can I stay at home unmarried without people becoming suspicious?"

He gawked offended. "You're going to abandon the family? You think I'm going to allow you to go to another state without me? That's not happening," he snapped, slashing his hand in air.

In response, she could feel her apricot skin growing crimson in anger. She wasn't abandoning anyone. She had every right to live her life. "I'll come back home for all the holidays. I just want to experience life a little and maybe even find my brother."

"So, this is what all the fuss is about? You want to find your twin brother and then what? We're your family. Maddison, Tory, Jason, my parents, my brother and his family, and I are your family. Why isn't that enough for you? Why be selfish and ungrateful? If your twin cared about you, then why hasn't he sought you out? I'm the only one who loves you. When will you understand that?" he fumed.

Virtuous bit the inside of her jaw and dropped her head, hating how he spoke to her but not idiotic enough to refute him. However, she wasn't ungrateful or selfish. If she was either of those things, she would have runaway a long time ago, but she stayed for Maddison and Tory, and it looked like she was going to have to continue to stay. Like a good and obedient child, she appeased him and apologized. "I'm sorry. I wasn't intending to be selfish or ungrateful. It was just a thought," she replied lowly, keeping her eyes low as not to intensify an already strained situation. "Please forgive me." As soon as the words left her mouth, he pulled her toward him and seized her lips. It wasn't a passionate kiss, at least not on her end. Once the kiss was broken, he hugged her body to his.

"Baby, I forgive you. I just love you so much and the idea of you leaving me is too much to bear. I know things are hectic with Addison acting out and the shift in the house, but you're strong and you can handle it. Do you love me?"

"Yes." The lie was automatic. The lie was survival, but it wouldn't be like that forever, she hoped. Every single day she prayed to God sometimes several prayers to Him to release her from her imprisonment.

"Good. When we get home tonight, I want you to show me how much."

Those words made her want to vomit, but she just shook her head. At least Addison had gotten her on birth control pills unbeknownst to Greg. The last thing she wanted to do was bring another child in the world for him to hurt.

A &Ω

Thunder woke Theory from a dead sleep, which was more like an unwanted nightmare. He was reliving the night he'd robbed the woman. Then that merged into how his parents had abused and neglected of him and ended with Staci and Noc. He was happy to be awake.

Theory wasn't afraid of storms. He liked them. They were soothing in their own way. Grammy used to tell them when there were thunderstorms to sit on the couch and be quiet, turn off everything, and let the Lord do His work. He quietly chuckled at the memory.

Instead of going back to sleep, he slid his feet into his thong sandals reached down and picked up his puppy Logic out of his crate and headed outside to sit the porch. He crept silently out of the house and eased into the black rocking chair and gently placed Logic in his lap. Apparently, his pup didn't have the same love affair with storms like him. He extended his long legs to the porch railing, lifted his head back and closed his eyes. This was comforting. It was like laying under a childhood blanket.

Theory inhaled slowly the fresh rain scent and a smile eased across his face. This would always sooth him as a child when his parents were too busy and forgot he existed. He let out a confused sigh. He didn't know why his mind was reliving the past he tried so hard to bury alive. He wanted to be completely free of his past and never allow his mind to cross that path again.

"I knew you'd be out here," Val's voice whispered, causing Theory to open his eyes.

"Whatchu doing out here? You need to put a shirt on out here, showing off that bird chest. You gonna mess around and get pneumonia," Theory joked, sounding like Grammy.

Val just shrugged his shoulders and eased down on the other rocker.

"What's on your mind, Val?"

"Nothing. I'm just happy you're back home. I mean Arch, Shalamar, and Trek took care of me, but you know it wasn't the same as having my big brother. Besides, nobody else understands why when it storms, I prefer to be outside."

"Why?" Theory asked, looking over at him.

"It's what you do. You know I wanted to be just like you," Val confessed.

That choked Theory up for a moment because the only legacy he'd left behind before being locked up was how to get in trouble. His mind was so messed up because of his background that...he didn't finish the thought.

"I'm doing my best to set a better example for you now. Black men have it a lot harder than most because of our skin color and because people would rather see us as thugs or entertainment and not engineers, presidents, or equals. So, never be the guy I was or our fathers, but be the man that God created *you* to be. Seek to be Christ-like not like man or me. I'll mess up. I'm trying my best not to, but at the end of the day I'm imperfect and my demons aren't all conquered. But you have my word I'll never leave you and Grammy like that again," Theory vowed.

It was silent after that. The only sounds were the steady thumping of rain and the roaring sound of thunder. Theo and Val were lost in their own contemplations. After another fifteen minutes, Val spoke, "Theo, do you ever think about your parents? I mean sometimes, I think about mine, my biological ones and my adoptive ones. I wonder what was so unappealing about me that both sets of my parents left me."

That wasn't what Theory had expected him to say, but he understood. Had he not been selfish, he would have been around for Val and let him know that he was the best kid ever. "I guess you want to get deep." When Val didn't answer, he looked over at him and saw his eyes were a little watery.

"Val, this I know for sure. You're an outstanding young man who has overcome so many obstacles. Not only are you a top athlete, but you are an A student. Universities are recruiting you. You're brilliant and you are a young man of God.

"You took care of Grammy when I was locked up and you have faith, I hope to one day have. You're responsible, motivated, smart, loyal and a good-hearted soul. You're what every parent prays their child will be. Uncle Gerald just let his PTSD take over and Sherry just got lost in the shuffle, but you're a great kid. I admire you. I always have and always will. Don't think of them as abandoning you. Think of it as

God protecting you. He knew that Grammy and Pops, Lord rest his soul, could provide better."

Theory watched him digest the words. "Is that what you do?"

Now, it was his turn to get watery eyed. Theory missed his parents, even though he disliked them. He knew how Val felt. It was deeply devastating to know his parents didn't want him. That's where his anger stemmed from. "Not at first. In the beginning, I was hurt. My parents neglected and abused me. I'd be hungry but there was no food to eat or anything to drink. I'd wake up to bedbugs and roaches using me as a meal or a roadway. I was like three or four then. That messes with your mental, you know. When it rained that was how I bathe and drank. When your parents stay high that's all they're concerned with, getting the next high. Then the money ran out and my parents happily gave me over to their dealer. Thank God he had a conscience and went to our grandparents or who knows where I'd be.

"The damage was done. I was fury on wheels, pissed at the world, but all that was to hide the shame and the pain of feeling rejected by my parents. I held on to the anger. You know the rest and I wish I could go back in time and change it all. Especially mugging that poor lady. You know I was high that night. First and last time I ever did drugs and there I was robbing some poor lady. I can't even really recall what I did. I've begged God for forgiveness," he confessed.

"God forgave you for sure and we did too. I was mad at you for leaving me. I felt like you abandoned me like my mom and dad, but Grammy explained it wasn't like that. That everyone deals with their suffering differently and that was how you had to work through yours. Me, I just put it in sports and academics. I thought if I was the perfect kid, they'd come back. My parents didn't come back, but you did. Don't ever leave me again," Val admonished.

"Never, little bro," he promised and stood up and pulled Val into a hug. "You know I love you and I'm proud of you, right? If you ever need to talk to me about anything, I'll always listen. One thing I learned in juvie, everybody needs someone to listen and the weakest men aren't those who cry and ask for help, it's the ones who think they can do it alone. Even Jesus had the angels minister to Him after Satan failed at tempting him. Never be ashamed of how you feel. Real men show emotions only cowards hide."

"I love you too," Val mumbled.

"C'mon, man. It's lightning out here. It's time to go back in the house."

"Yeah, good talk, Theo."

"Likewise," Theory replied. He really felt like a load had been lifted. He knew that God had good things in store for them. He said a prayer of thanksgiving, picked up a whining Logic, and headed back into the house.

A &Ω

One week later, Theory was a working man, and he enjoyed his job. He still hadn't heard from Vivi and figured her father must have found his number, but that was life. He had other things to be concerned about and to celebrate. He had been hired at Westinghouse and it was a good job with a lot of growth potential. He planned on saving as much money as he could for school.

Theory made sure to be proactive and went to visit Spartanburg Methodist College where he'd talked to an admission counselor. He was set to take the SAT soon and he knew his high school grades were good. He decided he wanted to pursue a degree in Engineering or Business. He was sure he would get into college there, then transfer elsewhere more than likely wherever Val would get a scholarship to play sports and they'd just move Grammy with them.

As Theory pulled up to his house, he let out an exhaustive but happy sigh. He was so thankful to have a job, to not be locked up and to have a family who had his back. That was the greatest feeling ever. Just as he opened his door his cellphone went off and he picked it up.

"Yo?"

"Theo, it's Trek. I meant to call you last week, but I was deejaying out of state and had a different venue about every night. Anyway, guess who was asking 'bout you."

"It better not be Staci, cuzzo. I already done told her what it is and she ain't it for me. It better not be Noc coming at me about Staci either. He don't want it. I'm good on that disloyal fake pair."

Trek burst into laughter. "Nah, not her but Congo and 'em. I told them you weren't into that life and was heading to college and doing big things."

"So, why I feel like that ain't sitting well with Noc?"

"Yeah, so, Noc was talking about your fighting skills and wanted to know if you wanted to fight for him. Since he got another kid on the way, he tryna transition out of the drug business into something less lethal, but still lucrative. His interest are now in fighting, gambling and opening a gym, don't know the particulars but he asked me to reach out so I am.

"My advice is to leave that mess alone. Ain't none of us Campbell men about that illegal life. It just ruins us, you saw what it did to your folks and Val's parents. I straight up told him you wouldn't be interested, but I would run it by you."

Theory had to chuckle at the gall of Noc. Dude had taken his woman, which he couldn't care less about now. No doubt they were messing around with each other while he and Staci were together and now, he was asking to make bread off his fighting ability. "That's freaking hilarious. Like what I look like working for him when he took my girl then knocked her up and got her strutting around looking like an ashy weather-beaten Zombie. Nah, I'm good with my job at Westinghouse. Tell Noc to do what he did when I was locked up, forget I exist. Ain't nobody pressed for his attention."

"I hear that. Do you have the weekend off? I want y'all to come to my show."

"Yeah, I just work Monday through Friday."

"That's what's up. I'ma make sure Val can come too."

"Cool. Well, let me get off this phone. I'm hungry and Grammy done messed around and made a macaroni pie, greens, baked pork chops with gravy, and mash potatoes. I'm 'bout to murder that meal."

"A'ight. Love you, man and I'm proud of you. Congrats on the new job. That's what I'm talkin' bout!"

"I'm a Campbell. It's what we do. Plus, it helped that Grammy's friend at church works at the same place."

"Right. Bye, bruh."

"Bye," Theory replied as he exited his truck and headed inside the house for his Grammy's good cooking and play with his puppy. Nothing was better than having the freedom to do what he wanted, and there was no way he was going backwards or be pulled back in to the world of darkness that Nocturnal lived in. He was forever done with that life.

A &Ω

A week later, Theory pulled up at the gas station. He and Archie were headed to link up with Trek. They hadn't long left the church where he had helped cut the grass and do some landscaping. He really enjoyed attending the services and volunteered to do the work since the guy that usually does it was out of town attending to a family matter.

"Yo, Theo, did you ever hear from that girl you were checking for in Gaffney?"

"Nope. I starting to get a complex. Maybe I'm too much for her."

"She did give off that scary vibe. Gotta watch chicks like that. They'll have you caught up. You probably dodged a bullet."

Theory chuckled, but he really did wonder about what had happen to her. Maybe it wasn't meant to be. "Archie, you want anything out the store?" he queried quick to change the subject.

"Yeah get me a Pepsi and a snicker bar. I'll pump the gas."

"A'ight," Theory replied and headed into the store. He sauntered toward the drinks. He wasn't a fan of soda, but he was into the Bai drinks that Val liked. Val was a real health conscious and was making Theory that way too. He retrieved Archie's drink of choice as he was backing out to get his own, he bumped into someone. He pivoted to excuse himself then noticed it was a girl but not any girl, it was *the* girl. Vivi was just as beautiful as before in all her natural glory, sporting cute cargo pants and a simple V-neck shirt. "Excuse me,Vivi," he stated, not believing that he was just talking about her and here she was in the flesh, looking and smelling good. When her eyes fixated on him her facial expression was one of alarm, and she paled as if she'd seen a ghost. Her reaction threw him for a loop.

"It's Theo," Maddison stated with a smile. "Hey, Theo. We missed you."

"Hey, cutie. I see you have better manners than your sister," he teased, tapping the tip of her little nose.

"Hey," Virtuous replied timidly.

"We meet again. It must be fate."

Vivi looked around the store as if someone was about to come over. It was then he noticed that her shyness had turned into fear. It made him nervous. Did she have a dude? He started looking around as well. "Vivi, you got a man or something. You're acting a little different. Look, you don't have to be afraid of me. I'on mean you no harm. As a matter of fact, I was just leaving." Theory didn't have time for this.

He could deal with shy, but scary was a level he didn't communicate on.

"No, I mean, I'm sorry." She let out a hard breath and ran her hand down her makeup-free face. "It's not you. It's my dad. He's in a rush and I don't want to get in trouble for being in here too long. If it's okay with you, I mean if, um, you're still interested in me. I mean if you're okay with me calling you, I'd like..." she stopped, apparently flustered. Her cheeks were red with embarrassment and she was fidgeting with her fingers and rocking side to side nervously. Theory knew he was an attractive guy, but he never made a woman act like this.

"Vivi, I ain't stressed. If you want to call me, then that's cool and if not, that's cool too," he lied.

She nodded and then grabbed Maddison's hand and ambled away, but not before he heard her mutter that she was so stupid and she had blown it. Before he could think, he reached out and pulled her back to him. Touching her sent a chill through his body like her energy was pulsating through him and it shocked him, but he liked it. "You're not stupid. I mean I get it, I'm a handsome guy, so if I were you, I'd get flustered too. It's cool, seriously," he joked.

"I'm usually not like this. I swear. I'd like to get to know you."

"Okay, Vivi, the ball is in your court." Theory winked at her and at Maddison and then walked away, but he could feel her eyes on him. He was going to get her for sure. Ladies like that were worth the wait. He kind of liked her awkwardness. He hummed a little tune as he gathered his items and paid.

Chapter 7

Addison was close to having a nervous breakdown. She thought she would outsmart her husband and go see her children at school, only to find out she couldn't. The look the school administrator gave her made her want to crawl under the biggest rock and die. She almost gave up until Greg had her served not once, but twice at her job. One was an order of protection and the other was legal separation papers and that just humiliated her beyond belief, but instead of letting anger win, she decided to get even.

Addison watched the house like a lynx, and she was sure that Greg was cocky enough not to change the locks or the security code on the house. She'd thought he let her come back home, but it'd been a week and all she saw him doing was putting more energy into his relationship with Virtuous and acting like his own wife never existed.

Addison was aware that some of her anger was misplaced, but she still hated Virtuous because at thirteen, she could satisfy Greg in ways Addison never had. Even when Virtuous implored her to intervene, crying until Addison thought she would drown in her own tears, she did nothing. Addison feared Greg too.

For years, she dealt with his transgressions by using drugs and leaving Vivi to fight her own battle, but now, Addison was pissed too. If Greg was allowing Addison to live in the house and they acted like a family, then she was fine. Addison let him do as he pleased, and she did as well, but this separation and him wanting a divorce was not sitting well with her. Either they went back to how it was, or she was going to make his life as miserable as possible.

Taking a deep breath, she exited the car under the cover of the moonless night and made her way to the two-story home that used to be hers. She missed Maddison and Tory, even though Virtuous took care of them most of the time, they were still her children. She had a right to see them.

Once she made it to the yard, she pulled out her house key and put it into the lock, but it didn't work. Angered, she crept around the back toward the double door entrance through the patio and used her key. It worked.

Addison stalked in and shook her head. Virtuous ran the house better than she ever had. Addison hoped once she was kicked out the home that the routine would fall apart, but that wasn't the case. It only made her feel like less than a woman, wife, and mother. Her own daughter was better at being domestic than she was. The jealousy she shouldn't have raised violently through her veins. How could a girl who had been abused for years have her life more together than Addison?

On the counter was a freshly homemade cinnamon bundt cake. It was perfect. It smelled heavenly. Livid by the picture-perfect scenery, Addison picked up the cake and tore it to pieces before throwing it all on the floor. That didn't relieve the pulsating acrimony or jealousy. No, she needed to do more destruction in her semi-drugged state of mind. She headed toward the refrigerator and opened it and found that Virtuous had prepared lunch for Maddison, Jason, Greg and Tory, which infuriated her more. This was her freaking family and Virtuous had stolen her life. She felt tears form and her face grew white hot. Virtuous was replacing her, and she knew the only way to get back her status was to take out her competition. Virtuous had to be eliminated.

Deciding that was necessary, Addison shut the fridge and promenaded over the locked drawer that held the knives. It was Virtuous' idea to lock up the sharp objects, so Maddison wouldn't accidentally hurt herself and Greg fell all over the idea like the girl was a genius. She grabbed the canister that was on the tabletop and got the key to unlock the drawer. She was so into what she was doing that she didn't notice someone approaching.

"Addy, how did you get in here?"

The male voice startled her, but she calmed when she saw it was only Jason. "This is my home. Don't call me Addy. I'm still your mother. I have a right to be here, so go back to bed Jay."

"Daddy said you can't be here anymore. He said you hurt the family. You have to go."

She stopped what she was doing and faced her nineteen-year-old nephew that she had adopted years ago. How dare he, her blood, choose Greg over her? "Go to bed."

"Get out," he warned.

"No," she snapped defiant, eyes glowing a deranged red.

Then Jason shouted for Greg to come and it was like the crazy spell she was under snapped and she ran out of the house like she was being chased by hellhounds. Addison was mental, but she wasn't stupid. She wouldn't die by Greg's hands. By the time, she ran around the front all the lights were being turned on and Greg opened the front door and came after her.

The loud breathing and the pounding of footfalls behind her sounding like a herd of buffalo let her know that he was close. Too close. Exerting the last piece of energy, she had, she attempted a gazelle like leap but he tackled her in midair down to the ground causing her to go dizzy with pain as the hard contact knocked the wind out of her.

Greg's larger body was hot with anger, he had an anaconda like grip on her making her fight for each breath that she took, their eyes clashed, rage in his, fear in hers. She should have planned this better, in was like in that moment she could see her past and present.

"What is wrong with you, Addy? You come in my home and you stress out my family after you've been carrying on an affair and attacked Virtue? You really want me to end you, don't you?"

"I'm sorry, Greg. Please, I just want my family back. I'll even let you keep seeing Virtuous," she tearfully replied.

"*Let me?*" he queried with a deep chuckle causing her fear to switch to fury. What was it about Virtuous that had him so warped?

"Daddy?"

"It's okay, Jay. Get the girls settled and I'm going to escort Addy off the grounds." He did just that. "I took your keys and I changed the locks, so how did you get into my home?"

"It's our home and you didn't change the backdoor lock."

"My name is on the paperwork. You know what? It doesn't matter. I'm calling the police to get this documented. You know you're not getting custody of the kids, right? You're making this so easy that they won't even get supervised visitation."

"Why do you hate me, Greg?"

"The same reason you hate yourself. Now, leave my house and stay away from my family. You come around again, and I'll put that stand your ground law to good use!" he roared and pushed her away.

It wasn't over. All Greg did was make her more determined. He loved Virtuous, well she would make him see what hurt felt like when she ended Virtuous' existence. She was going to have to deal with Virtuous now and expose Greg's dirty little secret.

Chapter 8

*V*irtuous grinned when she saw her best friend, Tamari. She was a beautiful girl. Her dark, milky smooth, complexion would make anyone jealous. She was a tall, thick and curvy size twelve. They'd met in the first grade and had been inseparable ever since. Tamari's father was a police officer too, which was why Greg didn't object to their friendship.

Tamari was asking about an update on Addison when a few of the football players arrived at their table. It was Kasen. He was built like a typical running back, lean muscle like a cheetah and just as fast. He was just an inch or two under six feet and was in the beginning stages of growing a goatee. His skin was the color of cocoa mix. He rocked a low fade with massive waves. He was super timid, but an all-around good Christian guy.

Then there was Cary. He was the kicker for the football team and a star soccer player. He had blonde hair and crystal gray eyes. He was over six feet tall. He was a party boy, but he was also Uncle Norman's son, so Virtuous never said a word about his partying. Plus, he had her back if anyone ever came at her wrong.

Bringing up the rear was Jerónimo, but everyone called him Nimo. He was the quarterback, extremely handsome with his olive toned skin, raven colored hair and piercing caramel eyes. He was half-Venezuelan and half-Puerto Rican and one hundred percent the guy all the girls wanted. He wasn't as wild as Cary or as studious and shy as Kasen. He was in the middle, but always cooler than a cucumber. There was a rumor around school that Nimo had a crush on Virtuous and Kasen was sweet on Tamari, but neither had said anything to either of the girls. So, they didn't comment and just chalked it up to high school banter.

The guys did this at least three times a week. It was strange when it first started happening because neither Tamari nor Virtuous were on the dance team, cheerleaders, or what people would consider *it girls*. Like jocks usually went for that type of girl, they were Christian girls. However, Tamari was a student trainer who assisted the team trainer when players got injured so she traveled with the team, but the only connection that Virtuous had was that she helped with Fellow Christian Athletes.

Other than that, she and Tamari were considered nerds because of all the academic clubs they were in. No one bullied them though and that was more than likely because of Greg. He was popular with the students as well as the staff and faculty. Like everyone loved him, which was why she'd never told anyone about the monster he could be. They would never believe her.

They all smiled and sat down on the other side of the table placing their trays down.

"Hey, there three amigos. Are you guys ever not together?" Tamari teased as they got settled.

"Hey, dope duo. Are you two ever not together?" Cary countered.

"Touché," Tamari replied.

While the two of them talked, Virtuous felt eyes on her and turned to see Nimo eyeing her. She dropped her head back to her salad.

"Vivi, are you coming to the varsity game Friday? We missed you last week," Nimo's strong tenor voice hummed.

"Who told you I wasn't there?"

"Vivi you sit in the same place every home game with Maddison and Tory decked out in school colors," Cary cut in.

"Well, I'll be there this week. Daddy is working so we all have to come anyway."

Nimo smiled. "You think your dad will let you hang out after?"

"Probably not."

"How about Saturday then? I mean we can all go as a group," he quickly stated as Cary started to act silly and make faces at him.

"I'll have to ask." It shouldn't be a problem, but Greg was one jealous dude and she didn't want to incur his wrath if she could avoid it. She was so scared after Theory talked to her in the store but thankfully Greg had saw a police buddy and wasn't paying her any attention at the time.

"Ask me what?" Greg asked as he stepped behind Vivi and placed his hands protectively, well more like possessively over her shoulders. Other kids were calling out to him and he addressed them briefly but kept his attention on her.

"Uncle Greg, can Virtuous spend Saturday night with me? I want her to go with me to visit my cousin's church." Tamari asked.

"Let me think about it. I'm not sure if this weekend will be good," he replied.

Virtuous was crestfallen, but she shouldn't be knowing that was how he operated. He liked to be where she was or at least have Jason around. If she could go anywhere, she'd be calling Theory and hanging out with him, but as it stood that was nearly impossible because Greg would never permit her to be around another guy.

"Well, would you mind if Vivi went out with us, like a group thing to Ruby Tuesday and to the movies on the east side of Spartanburg?" Nimo asked.

Virtuous could feel Greg's mind vellicating as he attempted an excuse to say no. He didn't like when guys talked to her let alone allow her to go out even in a group setting.

"Yeah, we're sure to win our game Friday and we like to celebrate. It'll be early, so we'll have her home in case you need help with Tory and Maddison." Cary assured.

"Let me think about it," he replied and leaned down and kissed the top of Virtuous head and gave Tamari a gentle pat on the back before walking away.

"Uncle Greg needs to chill. You're seventeen and this is your senior year. When is he going to allow you some freedom? It's not like I can corrupt you. I've tried and fail," Cary teased.

They all laughed.

A &Ω

At the end of the school day, Virtuous was headed to Greg's office. She was a little late but hoped he wouldn't be upset. She and Tamari were trying to come up with a plan to hang out for the weekend because her life was about to get seriously busy because of her senior art exhibit.

Virtuous really needed a break from the chaos that she called life. It saddened her that she couldn't share meeting Theory with Tamari, but it had to be that way to keep everyone safe. She really wanted to call Theory, he'd been on her mind heavy, but the consequences of that could be astronomical. Guh, she hated her life sometimes. She could really see herself dating Theory if not for Greg. She'd just add that to her prayers. If Theory was meant for her, God would make a way.

By the time she arrived at his office, something felt off. She wasn't sure why, but she got an ominous feeling like something wasn't right. She slowed her pace as she padded to the door and heard whispering voices. She was unable to piece together the conversation, but fear forced her forward. She knew that if Greg didn't see her face that would cause her problems. She cracked the door and gasped at the sight in front of her. Sandy, the senior guidance counselor was cleaning herself up while Greg was zipping up his pants. Not that she cared, because if he was doing that with Sandy, she hoped to God that he would leave her alone, but to do that type of thing at school was ridiculous and irresponsible. It was almost like he wanted her to see them.

Without saying a word, she shut the door and ran. She could hear Greg calling her name, but she didn't stop. She had to play this for her benefit. If she had learned anything from Addison, it was to use Greg's mishaps and mistakes to get what she wanted. For her, it was her freedom.

Virtuous reached her SUV and hopped in and drove to get Maddison. After that, she would pick up Tory and head to LeAnn's farm. She burnt rubber pulling out of the student parking lot and headed to Maddison's school. On her way there Greg continuously called her cellphone, but she ignored it. She was thanking God that she might get away from him finally. If this worked, she was sending Sandy a thank you note.

After picking up Maddison and sending a prayer of thanks to God that Greg hadn't followed her there, she headed to the daycare where Tory was. Her phone was still going off, so she put it on mute and to focus on driving. Once she arrived at the daycare, she unbuckled Maddison and helped her out of the SUV then the pair headed into the daycare.

As soon as they made it to the sidewalk, Virtuous was hit from the back, it was a hard blow that nearly knocked her out, but Maddison's screams kept her from giving into the soaring pain that ran rampant throughout her body. Virtuous immediately went into protective mode. Maddison fell as the attacker attempted to separate the two, but Virtuous pulled Maddison into her body and became a human shield while protecting her head as the female voice shouted to give her back her children.

That was when Virtuous knew that it was Addison, and from her deranged voice and crazy actions, she knew the woman was high, but she didn't think it was meth she was on this time. "Stop, please!" Virtuous shouted, tears forming as Addison stomped her and pulled her hair. She was unable to defend herself for fear that Maddison would get hurt, but when Addison's balled fist punched the side of her face, she was ready to go feral. There was only so much abuse she was willing to accept.

"Ma'am, get off her!" an unknown male voice yelled as he yanked Addison back.

It was all chaotic, there was screaming and cursing, but all Virtuous tried to fixate on was keeping Maddison safe. Then warm arms reached for her, causing her to jump in fear of another assault. "Virtuous, honey, come with me, let's get you out of here. Ms. Tyler is phoning the police now," Bev told her.

Carefully and painfully, Virtuous stood up with the assistance of Bev. Then she reached to help Maddison who was sobbing uncontrollably and bleeding from her knees. In the background, she could hear Addison screaming, "I want my children! I hate you, Virtuous. I'm gonna kill you! Let me go." Virtuous ignored her. Her head ached, her body was sore, and felt like she was on the verge of passing out. She couldn't really hear out of her left ear. She limped into the safety of the daycare and somehow, she managed to pick up Maddison and carry her inside.

"Where is Tory, Bev? Is she safe?"

"Yes, but you're bleeding badly so just sit, okay? I'll get Tory. The police are coming and so is an ambulance."

"Okay, call Mamaw LeAnn please."

Bev nodded and jumped into action, while the other parents who had looked on in horror, slowly overcame their shock and then attempted to help her and Maddison.

A & Ω

Greg arrived at the hospital a heat wave of anger was pulsating off him. Once his eyes landed on his daughters, he was even more enraged. Maddison was in tears and she had bandages on both knees. Her tiny body was wrapped protectively in her father's arms. Tory was wailing and flapping her little arms while Greg's mother attempted to calm her. He went right to Tory to soothe her and she calmed as soon as she heard his voice.

"Daddy, Mommy tried to take me and hurt Vivi. I'm scared," Maddison explained when Greg sat in the chair beside her looking over her wounds.

"I know baby, but there's nothing to be afraid of. Daddy won't let anyone hurt you or your sisters," he assured her before turning his attention to his mother. "Mom, where's Virtue. I need to see her."

"Of course, they're going to let her come home today. They wanted to keep her overnight, but she fussed and fought about having to keep Maddison and Tory safe. Poor baby... She was more worried about them than she was herself. I told her that the children would be fine, but she just wasn't hearing it."

"Okay, just take me to her. If they require her to stay then she will," he declared and followed his mom to the treatment room where she was being held. Greg's mother entered the room first, and he followed. Virtuous' facial expression was dead when she saw him, but it lit up when Tory fought to get out of his arms to come to her.

"Mom told me that you have told the doctors you refuse to stay, but you're not of age to be making that decision, so if they want you to stay you, will."

Virtuous didn't reply. She simply turned her attention to Tory. After five minutes, she spoke, "Mamaw, when I'm discharged, I want to go home with you. I think we'll be safer."

There was silence, but Greg was incensed at her attempt to disobey him. She knew he didn't accept that.

"Virtue—"

The doctor arrived before Greg could finish his sentence. He explained that the test had come back and that they were comfortable allowing her to leave the hospital, but to follow up with her primary care physician.

After the doctor left, Greg lifted Tory out of Virtuous' arms and handed her back to his mother, dismissing them before turning his attention back to Virtuous. He turned and sauntered over slowly and with purpose, his electric eyes never leaving her eyes. He could see her become nervous by the unknown. She was contemplating if her telling him what she was thinking could bring forth a violent reaction or one of calm. The uncertainty caused tension and anxiety to rise. Had she pushed him too far or had her act of disobedience excited his darkness? However, he liked seeing her in this state.

Greg gave nothing away as he leaned over the bed and reached out to run his fingers through her unbraided hair. It was wild after what she had suffered, and her pouty lips that he loved to kiss were chapped, but she was still beautiful, his beautiful obsession. He leaned down to her ear, noticing but not commenting on the trembling of her body. His little rabbit was afraid. "Virtue, don't be ugly to me. I know what you saw at school today was upsetting and what Addison did was traumatic, but I'm still in charge. Never forget that. Give Daddy a kiss and apologize to me."

To his shock and dismay, she didn't move. She simply stared at him, her apricot skin laced with the day's assault, red and bruised. But she made no move to adhere to his request. Had he been incorrect in his assessment? Was it, lividness and not fear that he saw spark in her eyes?

A joker-like smile etched across his sun-kissed flesh, and his eyes hardened. "Try me, Virtue," he challenged, though it came out as an invitation. They both knew it was a warning. Just that quick her defiance diminished. That volcanic look in her innocent eyes disappeared, she licked her lips, he hoped in preparation to kiss him, but that was not to be as the nurse interrupted their silent communication.

Chapter 9

*I*t was dark, but not late. Stars exploded in the sky while a half-moon lingered, lighting a path to where Virtuous was sitting on her knees, hands clasp, head slowly lifting seeking the comfort that the night allowed. She had been released from the hospital and brought back to her grandparents' home, which was where she'd wanted to go. However, she was frightened and unable to sleep. Her mind was full of worry and despair. The only way to calm the anxiousness was prayer. That was exactly what she was doing. She had just finished a prayer, a cry to God where she lamented her soul.

Behind her were Tory and Maddison, sleeping soundly and safely in her bed. She prayed for safety and freedom. Virtuous was tired of being Addison's punching bag and being Greg's surrogate wife. Both her parents were unusually fixated on accosting her for their own sadistic pleasure. She didn't know how to stop it, which led to a feeling of helplessness that was alienating and distressing.

Greg was the police, a pillar of the community, and other than his misuse of her, he was an outstanding father, and she was just an unwanted kid abandoned by her biological parents. To the world, Greg was a saint, but she knew he was Satan full of sin and lust and for now, she was trapped. Her heart called out to her twin. She had no idea where he was, but she needed her brother to come for her. Tears slid down her sloped cheeks, kissing under her chin and falling to her nightgown. Her heart was still heavy, so she prayed some more.

"Please, God, forgive me my trespasses and forget me not. I don't know if You'll want me or anyone else wants me after what I've suffered but let me find my twin. I just want my family, my freedom, and to be able to maintain my faith through the storms that I'm facing now. Help me survive for Tory and Maddison and for Valor and for myself. I'm tired, Lord. I'm so tired. Let peace reign where pain has loomed for far too long. Let me be free. Let me know safety, love, and peace," she moaned. "I ask this in Jesus' name. Amen."

Then she lay prostrate, heart pounding so intensely that it sounded like the Kentucky Derby was going on inside her body. Her upper torso shook in torture. Greg hadn't come yet, and she hoped he wouldn't that he would respect his mother's house and not hurt her, but he was a selfish man. Forcing herself to sit up, she calmed her body, but she was too tired to get back to the bed. The beating, the stress, the fear of Greg's retaliation had zapped all her strength and energy. She just wanted to sleep and wake up as someone else in someplace else.

Virtuous' deep state of rumination was interrupted, the light from the hallway entered first, followed by a shadow—

his shadow. Without turning, she knew it was him, her hearing had perfected the cadence of his footfalls, and the rhythm of his breathing, both brought her displeasure and dread. He had arrived and so her punishment would ensue even though he was the one who was wrong. She didn't care about his escapades with Sandy, she would encourage it if it meant his hands never touched her body again.

Quickly, before she could blink or think he was lifting her in his powerful arms. Somehow, he had closed and locked the door. Now she was in his arms and he was ambulating over the recliner adjacent from the bed, his scarred and callus hands controlled her body once more. She remained muted and peaceful unsure of his mindset, but thankful that he hadn't jerked her around or hit her.

Greg was gentle, supportive and trying to persuade her to yield to him, he pulled her closer to his chest resting his head atop hers and letting them be in the moment. At some point, her tense body relaxed, and he exhaled a breath before speaking. "I'm sorry about Sandy. I did it on purpose. I didn't like how you were entertaining Nimo and I needed to know you cared about me. I wanted you to catch me with Sandy, so you could see how it feels when I see you speaking to other guys. I haven't forgotten that thug you met in Gaffney." He sneered coldly, all pretenses of kindness and support vanishing as the *other* Greg appeared.

Greg's hands were now squeezing her face, animosity shone in his evil eyes, flickering like a burning candle. She knew this game, the rules always the same. He wanted her. He never received the kiss he had requested at the hospital and now was acting like a sullen child. As much as she hated giving into his demands, it was safer. Lord knew Addison had done enough to her.

Survival. Virtuous played her submissive role and whimpered. Greg eased his hold until she was free from his grip. Silently, she asked God's forgiveness because she was about to lie, but this was a lie to survive, not for personal gain, not to hurt anyone, this was a lie to live. She only ever lied to survive.

"I'm sorry, Daddy. I love you," she hiccupped.

He sighed, as he began to unbind her braided hair. "Me too. I shouldn't have used Sandy like that, but I didn't know how to make you understand. I can't believe Addy, but at least she's in jail tonight."

"I'm scared to go home." That was the truth.

"I know. I think the girls are too. Well, Maddison is, so maybe another night here and I'll get all the locks changed in the doors and windows this time," he told her his thumb caressing her plump lips. Ever so easily he got closer and closer until their lips touched. "I love you so much, Virtue. I've been thinking about what you said, and I love you enough that we can go out of state if you want. That way we can be together out in the open and no one will bother us. At first, I thought you were trying to abandon us, but you just wanted us to be together," he finished, his eyes glowing with mirth and excitement.

Yeah, he was way off on the latter part, but hey, if that's what he chose to believe, then she wasn't going to say differently. The truth was, she had every intention of running from him. However, never let your left hand know what your right hand was doing. She would fall in line and allow him to think he was right.

"Can I love you tonight? I need you, baby."

It took every ounce of strength not to roll her eyes or let out an annoyed breath. This man had no shame, nor did he care about her. She kept that thought to herself. Instead, Virtuous softened her voice and spoke tenderly, "The girls are here, and this is Mamaw's house. On top of that, I'm sore. I just want to sleep."

"You sure it's not because of Sandy? I don't want her. I only want you," he assured, stroking the strains of her hair.

"No, I'm really sore."

He nodded and just burrowed her deeper into his embrace.

"Daddy, I'd like to sleep in bed with the girls."

"No, if I can't have you, then I'll hold you. I need you close to me tonight. I could have lost you. It would destroy me if anything ever happened to you."

She stiffened but didn't respond. Thinking that the conversation was moot, she started to close her eyes as all the happenings of the day descended upon her. She was completely exhausted, mentally and physically.

"Virtue..." His voice was husky, laced with lust and hunger.

"Mm?" she questioned incautiously.

"Who do you belong to? Who has ownership of your heart?"

Her body was starving for rest, and her mind was a bit muddled and the honest answer came without thought or insult, "God."

He growled and squeezed her roughly. "Take off your nightgown," he demanded in a biting whisper.

"What? Why?" she whined, not understanding what she had said or done wrong.

"You belong to *me*. Your heart is mine to own and no one else's, not even God. In this relationship, I am *God*. Take it off!"

Not able to fight, and though her body was sore she did as he'd ordered. His words terrified her. Had her mind began actively thinking, God knows she would have lied and said him. Her mind was just so exasperated and weary. She chastised herself for not playing the game right. Now, she would be punished. Just like all the times before he branded her body with his. While he showed his dominance, she prayed to God that her deliverance was coming soon. Her body wouldn't be able to continuously handle this kind of torture.

A & Ω

Val snapped out of his sleep, his heart was pounding, and his breathing was labored and erratic. He felt her, his twin. She was out there somewhere in pain. The connection was so strong that tears started to fall from his eyes. Not for the first time did he wish he and his sister had been adopted together. He didn't know where she was or who she was with, but he knew that she needed him. He felt it deep down in his soul. She needed him now, and there was nothing he could do, at least not yet. So, he did what Grammy always did no matter the situation. He hopped off his bed and prayed for his sister.

Unable to go back to sleep after praying, he headed to the den and turned on the television to see what was on. A news segment was starting, reporting something about a mother attacking her daughter and trying to kidnap the other one. He was so into the news that he didn't notice his cousin, Theory, entering.

"Whoa, these people be off the chain."

"Bruh, whatchu in here mumbling 'bout?" Theory queried, his puppy Logic came out to greet him.

"Hey, Theo. How was work?"

"It was straight. I like my job. Now, what were you talking about and why are you up this late?"

Valor lifted his brow questionably because he wanted to know what Theo was doing coming back home so late, but he didn't speak on it. "I was just watching this news segment about this lady who got arrested after attacking her daughter at the daycare and then trying to kidnap the other daughter."

"Word? I hope it ain't Black people."

"Nah, it wasn't *us* this time."

"Why you up, though? I know you not waiting on me." He was actually home late because he'd had some errands to run.

Val sighed and distress carved over his youthful facial features.

"What's up with that face? Did you get a girl pregnant? Best believe Grammy gonna beat you with the broom stick. She's not trying to be a great-granny."

"Bruh, don't even put that in the universe. It's nothing like that," he vowed, taking his hand and rubbing his face before looking Theo dead in his eyes. "You know I'm adopted, right?"

"Yeah, but that has never mattered. You're still my family. Why? Did somebody say something? If so, I'll handle them. You're a Campbell same as me."

"I know," Valor replied amusingly. "Nobody has ever made me feel any less, but I got a twin sister out there somewhere and I need to find her. I think, no, I *know* she's in trouble. I can feel it. It's like she calls out to me, but I can't reach her. It woke me out of a dead sleep. I prayed about it, but I'm still restless, scared even."

Theory grew serious after hearing that. "The twin bonds are real. Okay, let's research and contact DSS. Shoot, we can even reach out to a family law attorney. If there's anything I can do to help, I will. She's family too, and if you feel like she's in trouble, then we 'bout to be Black superheroes," Theory joked, making them both guffawed.

"Aye, I'm Black Panther and you can be Black Lightning," Val claimed.

"Nah, I'm the oldest, so I get to be Black Panther. Hello, he has an entire kingdom."

"Whatever. Let's eat. Grammy done messed around and made lemon pepper wings and loaded bacon potato wedges. They're good too. Then we got strawberry cake with pink lemonade."

"That's what's up. C'mon chop it up with me while I eat. Tomorrow, we'll start looking for your sister."

"Thanks, Theo."

"Always, little brother, always."

A & Ω

Virtuous woke up the next morning and she was in her bed, but the girls weren't. That didn't alarm her because she knew for a fact that Greg would never abuse his daughters. However, her body was still sensitive from his abuse and her head ached. She sluggishly slid off the bed and headed to the shower.

Each step was excruciating. Her mind instantly replayed the abuse of the night before and tears traveled relentlessly down her face. She felt trapped and so full of rage, but there was no way to release it. Greg was stronger than she'd ever be, and prayer just didn't seem to be the best defense. She was losing the battle. Shaking the depressive thoughts, she resumed her routine.

Virtuous shampooed and conditioned her hair and scrubbed her flesh, trying to wash Greg's sins off her body. Once done, she dried and dressed in fitted jogging pants and a V-neck T-shirt. She had no intention of attending school today and when she checked the time on her iPhone, she knew no one expected her to either.

Virtuous had a few messages from Tamari and Cary which, she answered. Apparently, the entire situation had been on the news, but her name wasn't revealed. However, someone had taken cellphone footage, which embarrassed her. Her face wasn't shown, but Addison's face was, so if anyone knew the family, they could put two and two together. Right now, her life sucked and it seemed to be getting progressively worse.

After how Greg had treated her body last night, she wanted revenge. God forgive her, but she had the deadliest thoughts against him. For years, he had abused her body at his will, made her the sex surrogate, and she was done with it. She didn't know how much more she could endure before she snapped.

The only way had she survived last night was by thinking of dark, rustic, soulful eyes, eyes that belonged to Theory. Not even her *World of all* or the girls had lulled her back. No, it had been *Theory*. He didn't even know he had become her saving grace. He'd given her something she thought she had lost a long time ago—hope. If that ever diminished, Greg would declare victory, and she didn't want to lose to him.

With that thought, she decided and hoped it wouldn't backfire on her to contact Theory. He was her one chance at normalcy. When a person had as much darkness in their life as she did, she needed light, and Theory, at least for now, would be her light. He made her want to sing "This Little Light of Mine." Taking a deep breath, she typed a message to Theory on her phone and sent it. She hadn't told a lie when she'd told him she had a photographic memory. She recalled everything about him such as his smell, his clothes, and even the curl of his eyelashes. Everything had been committed to memory.

Theory: Who dis?

Vivi: It's Vivi, Theory.

Theory: Oh, U remember ur boy now?

Vivi: I told you I have a photographic memory. Sorry, it took so long to reply, but my Daddy is my second skin and would be furious if he found out I contacted you. That's why I was acting strange in the convenience store.

Theory: Pop is doing the most huh? Wat up? You live in Sparkle City?

Vivi: Yes, in Boiling Springs.

Theory: WYD 2 day?

Vivi: Nothing, I'm playing hooky.

Theory: What? I got good girl vibes from you.

Vivi: I'm a good woman, not a girl.

Theory: LOL, right. I'm @ work, wanna do lunch @ Texas Roadhouse or meet up later this evening?

Vivi: Let me see if I can get away from my Dad.

Theory: Aye, don't get cha boy murdered :(

Vivi: Never. I'll hit you back later.

Vivi's heart was beating so rapidly that she could barely catch her breath. She was literally squealing with excitement. Never in her seventeen years had she been allowed to interact with the opposite sex. Greg just didn't accept competition, but now, she was going to meet a guy without Greg or Jason chaperoning her every step. Coming back to her good senses, she made sure to delete the entire thread just in case Greg decided to check her phone.

"Vivi, honey, are you up?" LeAnn questioned as she knocked on the door.

Still smiling from her excitement, she stood as LeAnn entered. "Yes, ma'am. Come on in."

LeAnn entered and Vivi greeted her with a smile. "You look happy."

"I am. Is my dad here?"

LeAnn pursed her thin red stained lips and then shook her head no. Virtuous suspected that LeAnn thought she would be disappointed at his absence, but she was thankful and one second from doing the Milly Rock. "No, honey, he went to work. He's collecting your homework and Maddison's for the remainder of the week. I told him you all needed some time off."

"Great. Do you think I can go to west side of Spartanburg? I have a taste for Texas Roadhouse and I'm low on my art supplies." All she wanted was to remove the memory of the devastation that Greg had inflicted upon her body last night with the girls right in the bed. It was a new sickening low that she didn't want to relive. What if they had woken up and saw what he was doing to her? That would have been catastrophic.

"Sure, I don't see why not. I keep telling Greg that he keeps you cooped up too much. He always has you babysitting your sisters. You are old enough and responsible enough to go out on your own." She shook her head as if she'd been exasperated by Greg's actions. She continued. "He did agree that you can start working at the farm again, but I know you want to spend time with your friends too. So, I'm going to speak to him again."

"Thanks, Mamaw, but can we keep my little outing between us? Daddy gets all mad for no reason and he'll blow it all out of proportion. My body can't take much more," she slipped.

LeAnn's bright eyes turned concern at Virtuous' confession, but thankfully her grandmother didn't speak on her latter statement. "Consider it done. My lips are sealed. Have fun, sweetheart."

That was why she loved her Mamaw. Once LeAnn left out of her room, Virtuous quickly texted Theory that she would meet him for lunch. It was beyond exciting to be able to go out and not be under Greg's thumb.

A few hours later, Virtuous, Maddison, and Tory pulled into the Texas Roadhouse parking lot. Virtuous was a little nervous when she left the house for several reasons. One, Greg might call and discover her gone, and two, Theory might see how awkward she was and never want to see her again. She said a little prayer to God and did her best to turn off her insecurity and awkwardness. This was her first outing with a guy, and she wanted it to go well.

Theory was cool about her bringing the girls and she was thankful for that. That gave him extra points. Virtuous was so enthused to be out on her own, and she was happier to have the girls with her. If they liked Theory, it would be a plus for him as well.

A last-minute emergency had come up that LeAnn had to tend to, which was why Virtuous had to bring them. Honestly, she loved having them around, so it didn't matter to her.

After what had occurred with Addison, she would have been worried about the girls not being with her. Virtuous didn't think that Addison would physically harm the children like she had done to her, but she also knew that Addison was incapable of taking care of the children. Looking in her rearview mirror, she checked on the girls who were in their own little world. Tory was currently sucking on her fingers and just steady talking to Maddison who was just as excited as Virtuous was to see Theory again.

Seeing that they were well entertained with each other, her mind went back to Theory. Virtuous hoped he wouldn't think she was lame because she had taken so long to contact him. She started to worry her bottom lip and what she and Theory would discuss during their lunch. She really loved his name. It was rare, kinda of like him and her too. She'd never met another Virtuous. As she parked her SUV, it hit her that she had no idea what kind of vehicle he drove.

A & Ω

Theory couldn't wait to see Vivi again. He was probably way too excited. This girl had him totally reneging on his idea to suppress his interest in pursuing women. However, he wanted to know Vivi better and if they just ended up being friends, then that would work too. He had just arrived and parked his truck. He pulled out his cellphone and dialed her number. She picked up after the first ring.

"Vivi, are you here?"

"Yes, the girls and I are in my SUV. We're getting out now."

"A'ight. I'm getting out my truck now too. I'll help you with your sisters."

"Great. Thank you."

Theory grinned. Virtuous was just sweet and polite, nothing like the females he used to run into before he got locked up, but he liked that about her. They hung up and he hopped out of his truck and looked around to see where she was. He spotted her easily. She had her hair pulled back into a slick ponytail. Sunglasses hid her pretty eyes. He strolled over to her SUV where she stood and little Maddison ran toward him.

"Maddy, be careful," Vivi admonished, but he waved her off. It was nice to have somebody that excited to see him. Theory thought cutie had forgotten all about him. Her over-the-top reaction made him feel good. "Calm down, she's good, Vivi. She made sure no cars were coming."

Carefully, Theory lifted Maddison up in his arms and then watched Vivi bend down and get her other sister. She also pulled out a large Brahmin tote bag. He guessed it held the baby's stuff. He believed she said the baby's name was Tory. However, what currently held his attention was the way her Polo dress was showcasing her toned legs. All three of sisters were wearing the same canary yellow. Normally, he wouldn't openly check her out, but the dress looked nice on her frame.

"Okay, are you ready?" Vivi asked him, nearly catching Theory checking her out.

"Yeah, let's go."

The pair started walking with Maddison still in Theory's arms with her arms wrapped securely around his neck. Tory was burrowed into Vivi. Theory just couldn't stop staring at her. They really looked like a young family. Theory opened the door for Virtuous to enter first. They were greeted by the hostess and he let her know how many were in the party. Theory noticed how the hostess stared at him.

Then it hit him. He was a large black man holding a white child and apparently, that was an oddity to her. *Why?* When transracial adoption was big in America, for all she knew, cutie could be his daughter. To her credit, she didn't speak on it and seemed to get over the initial shock. However, it could have been the mean mug he shot her as well.

Since they were a small party, they were quickly seated, and as they were escorted to their seats, there were stares. Theory noticed that Vivi did not comment on it, so neither did he. Little Maddison was still attached to him like a second skin. It was safe to say that she approved of him. Now, he had to get her other sister's approval and it would be all good.

"So, Vivi, are you in college?"

"No. I'm in my senior year of high school. You?"

"I'm applying to colleges," he replied. He had figured she was young, but not *that* young. He was twenty-one, so if she was a senior, she was seventeen or eighteen. If she was just seventeen, they'd have to be phone friends 'cause he wasn't getting caught up by her overprotective daddy. In South Carolina, the age of consent was sixteen years old, not that he was seeking a sexual relationship with her, but a lot of fathers would have an issue with a man his age wanting to date their teenage daughter.

"That's great. So, do you work at Westinghouse?" she queried, pointing at his shirt.

She was observant, and he liked that. "Yeah. I like it." Just as he spoke, the waitress came and took their orders and told them she'd be back with some bread. While they waited Theory cracked peanuts for himself and Maddison.

"Eat Ma-ma." Tory's gibberish, pulled Vivi's attention.

"Hold on. Let me get you a snack," Vivi replied and opened the large tote. Theory saw an activity book, clothes, a sippy cup, and a few other gadgets for kids.

Theory wanted to ask her if Tory was her daughter, but just as he fixed his mouth to do so, the bread arrived. He wasn't a bread man, but for real, he loved Texas Roadhouse rolls. He was about to pop it in his mouth when he heard someone call his name.

He glanced up and turned his nose all the way up. It was Nora Jean. *Why was she on this side of town? Didn't she have class or something?*

"Hello, Vicious," she greeted with a conniving grin that indicated she was up to no good. "Is this your girlfriend? You work quickly, don't you?"

Apparently, she wanted to see the vicious side of him. He sighed and then glanced around her to see if Maisha was with her, but he didn't see her, so he addressed Nora. "Nora, is it?"

"You know my name." she cooed flirtatiously as if doing so would upset Vivi. At least he hoped it didn't. He really disliked messy females.

Theory wasn't even having that a little bit. Why did women feel it necessary to approach a man that wasn't interested? She was trying to be trifling, but he wasn't in the mood. "Listen here, apparently you don't know me. I don't know your reason for coming over here bothering me and my friend but let me help you out. I don't care for you. Something about you screams troubled and desperate like you're way too eager for some attention that I'll never give you. Make this your last time approaching me. Step off and never step to me again. Walking around like you high class when you have no class."

She had the good sense to be embarrassed and ran off. He shook his head, annoyed before turning to look at a shocked Vivi. "I'm sorry about her. I don't even know that girl like that. I briefly met her when my cousins brought her to a family gathering and she's just salty because I kicked her out," he added.

"I wasn't going to speak on it, but thank you for explaining," she replied, her soft, melodious tone eased his annoyance with the situation and even caused him to smile.

"Well, Vivi, tell me about yourself."

She offered him a bashful grin before answering. "There's not much to tell. I go to school. I'm not in any sports, just the academic and art clubs. I like to draw and paint. I'm always with these two, and I'm active in my church. That's pretty much all of me."

"I like that. So, you don't have a boyfriend, not even a secret one?"

"Oh, my gosh, no." She blushed, and he knew she was telling the truth. "I've never been out with a guy until you. I hope that doesn't make me seem like a loser. It's just that my dad would kill me. I'm not allowed to even hang out with my guy friends even when said guy is my cousin."

"Seriously?" He shook his head. "No, you're not a loser." Theory scowled. Her daddy was on a new level of crazy. How could he not trust her to be around her cousin?

"Yeah. It's quite problematic, but I'll be in college soon. I need the freedom."

"Your old man is doing the most. That's bizarre that he acts like that. He needs to let you live," Theory expressed, but he could see that she didn't like talking about her overprotective dad, so he moved the conversation along. "Did you see the news last night? My brother told me that some lady attacked her daughter and then tried to kidnap the other one."

"That was our mommy," Maddison stated as a matter of fact and then showed Theory her knees. "I got two booboos, but Vivi had a lot of them. Didn't you, sissy? We had to go to the hospital. Daddy said mommy won't hurt us anymore and Vivi's Mom now."

Well, that was a wealth of information he was unsure how to file. When Theory looked at Vivi, her face was contorted as if she might have a stroke. Her beautiful skin was crimson now and her eyes were as wide and dark as a wormhole. He hoped she wasn't embarrassed. He knew about abuse and he wasn't judging. "I'm sorry to hear that. I guess that's why your dad is extra protective. Don't be embarrassed. I'd never judge your situation. My parents abused me as a child and my grandmother had to raise me. You and I are kindred spirits on that level." He had not meant to get that personal so fast, but it felt right to share that.

Virtuous dropped her head and Theory reached out his hand to lift her head back up. "You've got nothing to be ashamed of. Make sure you keep your head up always. Besides, you're too beautiful to hide. I promise you I don't view you differently. My Grammy says people who survive abuse are victors, not victims and their survival only adds to their value."

Virtuous offered Theory a timid smile and it lit his heart afire. She had him mushy. Who was this girl? How was he already bugging on her?

They chatted more and then their food arrived. Theory made sure that everyone clasped hands before he blessed the meal. He could tell that Vivi liked that too. He had some residual viciousness, but he was raised right and knew his beginning and ending.

Once they were done eating, Theory escorted them all back to Vivi's SUV and watched her snap the kids in. It was obvious that her sisters adored her. They interacted so well with one another. He could see the closeness between them just like it was between him and Valor.

"Can I see you again or call you?"

"I'd like that, Theory, but I have to be careful. My dad will lose it if he finds out I have a guy friend."

"I get it. Your old man is psycho. Let me get your phone, there are apps that will allow us to talk, and your dad won't ever know."

She did as he'd asked, and he fiddled with her phone. He really needed to hurry up before he was late getting back to work. "Okay, it's done. Where are you headed to after this?"

"I need to get some more art supplies and I promised Maddison one toy. Then we're headed back to Boiling Springs. Thank you for lunch and conversation, Theory. I enjoyed it."

"Any time, Vivi. Hey, what's Vivi short for?"

Her hazel eyes looked everywhere but his, she was stalling. "I don't want to tell you because you'll make fun of me."

"Don't play me like that, Vivi. I'm good and grown. I'd never make fun of you."

She rolled her eyes but finally told him. "It's Virtuous."

"Really?" He beamed. "I like that. It's unique and beautiful like you. It's definitely a fitting name."

"It used to be," she whispered.

Theory didn't have time to dissect that last sentence or the facial expression that followed, but he would later. "I think it's a beautiful name. Virtuous, I'll hit you up soon."

Theory opened the door for her to get inside and then waved goodbye to her sisters. Before shutting the door, he kissed her cheek and watched a fiery blush paint her face. "Bye Vivi, and thanks for meeting me for lunch.

"You're welcome and thanks for asking. I better go," she replied but wouldn't look him in the eyes. She was shy, but that was okay because he'd work on that. He shut her door and ambled away. Vivi was a mystery, but Theory would find out everything there was to know about her.

Chapter 10

*A*ddison was glad to see her mother and stepfather whom she hadn't spoken to in a while because they'd been estranged. She was thankful they had driven from Yemassee, SC, which was approximately a three-hour drive to bail her out.

It was a blessing they'd come to get her because she wasn't made for jail. Had she been thinking clearly, she would have never attacked Vivi in such a public setting. Now, she was sure she would probably lose her job.

"What were you trying to accomplish with that act Addy?" her mother questioned in a scolding tone. Her stepfather, Richard remained, silent. She knew it was his money that had gotten her out.

"I don't know. My life is just falling apart. After being served at work I went on a drug binge and my actions yesterday weren't calculated. I just lost it."

"You're going to rehab. I called your father, Tommy before I came here, and we agreed that you can go to the rehab center down in Savannah, Georgia. We've already buried one daughter, and I'd like not to bury another. And only God knows where Beatrice is," Makenzie replied.

If her mother had known Virtuous' identity or her genetic origin, she would have left Addison in jail. Virtuous and her twin brother, Valor, belonged to Addison's half-sister, Valerie. Valerie was her baby sister by her father. He had cheated on her mother with the maid who had skipped town and left her child. Her mother had never batted an eye even though she had given birth two years prior to her middle sister, Beatrice, who was Jason's no-good birth mother.

Beatrice was off being an old lady to some dude in a biker gang. Her mother had raised Valerie as if she were her daughter. Valerie never knew otherwise, and no one had ever told her the truth. But when she fell for a Black man who their father didn't approve of, their perfect family fell apart. Valerie got pregnant and Dad wanted her to have an abortion, but she'd chosen life, which was what Mom had wanted and that'd put a strain on the marriage. Her parents divorced and her sister gave birth, but Tommy did not know that. Valerie then gave up her children, abandoning them at a church.

Fast forward, she took in Virtuous, knowing her background. But she never told her sister. Addison blamed Valerie for their parents' divorce, her sister never knew about Virtuous. Then right around when Virtuous was about to turn twelve, her sister was robbed up in Anderson. Why she was there was a mystery. Then again, they'd been estranged for years. After that, Valerie suffered a heart attack from an overdose, which was bizarre because she had never done drugs. Of course, their father Tommy, had blamed it on the Black influence in her life.

Yes, Addison was attacking her own niece. Even Greg didn't know that Virtuous was her biological family. She did love Virtuous. She really did, until the child became her competition and did everything better than her. It was like being outdone by Valerie. Had Addison been smarter, she would have taken Valor, but Greg wanted a daughter so badly. At the time, all she wanted to do was please him.

"Did you hear me, Addy?" her mother's Southern drawl drew her back to the present.

"Yes, rehab... We just need to get Greg to drop the charges. Maybe Daddy or Richard can reach out to him because he doesn't want to hear from me."

"We'll see. Let's just get you out of here. I still can't believe you were attacking your own children. Is having four too many? You've seen the stress and mess that Beatrice caused with her running off with that biker gang. We loss Valerie untimely and now, you have this drug problem that has turned into child abuse. I swear y'all are trying to put me in an early grave."

"It was all a misunderstanding that I'll get a handle on." Being locked up was really an eye opener for her. She needed to get her life right.

"Really? Greg called me and told me a lot. He said you're stepping out on your marriage vows and that this was your second attack on your daughter. It's all on the local news. The only way you're going to get visitation with the children is to show that you are proactively seeking treatment. More than likely, you've lost Virtuous. I haven't seen that child in a long time. Hopefully, now, you'll let us see our grandchildren."

Addison said no more to her mother because she was right. The true villain in all this was *Greg*. He was the one who was sexually abusing their daughter and had chosen her over his wife, which had caused Addison to become seduced by drugs and another man. He deserved the blame too and since he wanted to call her out, maybe it was time to call him out as well. See how he liked having others knowing his dirty, dark secrets.

A & Ω

Virtuous hung up with Tamari who had called to check on her since she hadn't come back to school. For Virtuous, it had been her best day. It was the first day she smiled and didn't have to escape to her special place. A day without Greg had done her wonders. She sat back down at the desk and started drawing again. Normally, she illustrated a fantasy world, the place she escaped to whenever Greg was abusing her. Her *World of All*, where nothing but good things happened to all the inhabitants.

Today, she was drawing Theory. After he kissed her cheek, an explosion of unknown feelings and emotions erupted inside of her. It was like she was a walking heart-burst emoji. He had completely shattered her defenses. He was so welcoming and understanding. That had earned him recognition and a place in her queendom.

Virtuous had never drawn a man before. In her queendom, there were only females. Men, in her mind, devoured and destroyed the beauty of women. In her world, women ruled, and they were warriors. She was the warrior queen. She had dubbed Maddison and Tory her warrior princesses and they loved it. This, having Theory in her safe space, intrigued her. She never thought she would want a relationship whether it was friendship or more. Theory had proved himself worthy.

The song "I'm Yours" by Alessia Cara played and she could relate. She had not been looking for Theory, but he'd entered her life. She'd never looked to a man to be her salvation and save her from the arms of Greg. She wasn't naïve enough to believe that happy endings were reality and yet, she wanted Theory to be. She closed her eyes and as the song played her hands went on their own accord. She was in the moment, feeling the words, amazed that Theory had so effortlessly invaded her *World of All*. He was making her feel more artistic.

For her senior project in art, Virtuous had to do an art exhibit and for a while, she wasn't sure what she wanted to paint or title her show and now she had it. Virtuous was going to break the project up into three pieces that told the story of her life. Theory would be part of it.

Virtuous had it bad after one date or had lunch with her and her sister really been a date? At any rate, she was one hundred percent smitten with Theory as was Maddison.

Falling into the melody, she felt her hands go faster and then nothing. There was complete silence. Her eyes popped open and there was Greg. The glower in his eyes sucked her breath in an instant. In her mind, he was the reincarnation of the devil. Evil oozed out of his pours, proving her correct.

Her mind tried to escape. She could already imagine what he would do to her for leaving the house and having lunch with a man she was forbidden to see. His rough hands ran over her face finally settling under her chin. His grip wasn't unbearable, but more of a warning of his capabilities. *Did he know?*

"You've been naughty, Virtue," his twisted voice vibrated.

Utterly confused, she had no idea what that meant. Instead of falling prey to his game, she offered him her puppy-dog eyes followed by a clueless expression.

"You manipulated your grandmother into allowing you to leave today. You thought I wouldn't find out? If you weren't well enough to attend school, then how come you were able to venture to the west side?" he queried through clenched teeth.

"I needed art supplies." Then she gently placed her hand atop his to turn her head to show him what she'd purchased. "I didn't manipulate Mamaw. She said I should go out more. I didn't do anything wrong. I just spent time with Maddison and Tory. I wished I had taken them to the park as well. It's not healthy being in the house all the time. Daddy, please, you're hurting me."

Greg let out a heavy sigh and collapsed to his knees. "I'm sorry. I'm just in a bad mood," he replied.

Wasn't he always? Nothing inside of her wanted to comfort him. Whatever situation was irking him was done because of his need to control everything and everyone.

Greg placed his heavy hands on her thighs and started to rub up and down. Now that she was focused on his face, she could see that something was bothering him. "What's the matter?"

"Addison made bail. Her parents came to get her."

Virtuous gasped. "Why?"

"She has the right to make bail. It'll be okay."

Virtuous stiffened in real fear. How'd she get released so fast? Who were Addison's parents that they could do something like that? It didn't matter. She wasn't leaving the safety of Mamaw's house. "Well, I don't feel comfortable going back to your house. The girls and I will just stay here. I'll go back to school next week."

Greg's head popped up and his eyes darkened, causing Virtuous a moment of terror, but she remembered where she was, and he couldn't harm her here at least not too badly. "Virtue, I get the attack frightened and upset you. I know you're pissed off about me and Sandy, but you don't dictate what will or won't be to me. I let you stay out of school and you run one errand without me, or Jay and you think you're all grown up and that you run the show. Make the mistake that Addison did, and you'll get the same result. Stay in your place, Virtue, and that place is beneath me, serving me and doing what I say when I say it." He seethed, as he painfully clamped down on her thighs.

Virtuous swallowed a scream. Tears gathered in her eyes and raced down her cheeks, but Greg remained unmoved and his grip only tightened. She placed her smaller hands onto his and jerked them off. It felt like her skin had been separated from her leg muscles, but she quickly hopped up from her vulnerable position, attempting to make a run for it. Her actions caused him to topple to the floor, but he was faster.

He caught her by the waist and yanked her back, causing her to smack the wall hard and bounce off right into his chest.

"What was that, Virtue? Have you lost your mind?" he fumed, spit spewing out of his mouth as he spoke.

Virtuous refused to answer him or look in his eyes. Her heartbeat was thumping wildly, causing her difficulty in breathing. Of course, he wasn't having that so he back her into the corner, trapping her there before lifting her chin, forcing her to stare into his eyes. They were the color of an eclipse. She didn't have to look at him to know that. She could feel the malevolence overtake him.

"Baby, I'm sorry. Look at me please," he coaxed in a tender tone. This was how he tried to lure her in when he'd gone too far. When she was younger, she'd fall for it because all she wanted was to please her father, but not anymore. She knew better now. This was all part of his control and manipulation.

"No. Just let me stay here with Mamaw and Papaw. That way, you can have Sandy and Addison. I don't care. I want to enjoy my senior year and not get smacked around all the time. I've never done anything bad to you or Addison. I hold your secrets, I do what I'm told, and yet you two feel it's your right to threaten and abuse me. Leave me alone," she pleaded. Never had Virtuous been that courageous to speak out against her oppressors, but she deserved a life just like Mamaw had said.

"Virtuous, I told you I don't want Sandy and I'm sorry for that. It was stupid. You know I love you. I act out when you don't do what I ask, but you're right. You've never done anything bad and you don't deserve Addison's abuse. So, for the week, I'll let you stay here, but you're going to school. And I'll let you hang out with your friends this weekend. You can start back working on the farm. Now, let me see a smile. I hate when you look unhappy."

Virtuous wasn't sure she believed Greg. He would probably tell her anything to get her in line. Like was he really going to allow her to go out with Tamari? If so, that would be glorious because then she could talk to Theory. "You promise?"

"Yes, Virtue, I promise. I'm sorry I lost it for a second," he apologized, placing his forehead on hers, forcing her to gaze into his eyes. He lifted his thumb and caressed her bottom lip. "I won't ever do what I did with Sandy again. I just want *you*, Virtue," he pleaded, pulling her into an embrace. Then his honey-dripping tone altered into a darker warning tone. "Virtue, if I ever find out that you're messing around on me, you'll not like the consequences."

Virtuous stiffened. Her body became a board. Then somewhere she found her voice, small as it was, she spoke without hesitation, "And if you ever disrespect me again, you won't like my response." She didn't care about him or Sandy, but she wasn't about to let him get one up on her. In this life, survival meant playing Greg's game.

He did something that shocked her. He laughed full and hearty. "I was waiting for you to show me you cared. C'mon, the girls are outside. I want to spend some family time."

He'd hurt her. Her back was throbbing, but she was smart enough not to complain. Reluctantly, she followed him.

Chapter 11

S taci entered J Peters Grill & Bar. She wore a sundress and paired it with some flats and wore her hair naturally. She was meeting up with Maisha and Rika who were Vicious' cousins. Maisha's friend girl, Nora Jean, was with them. Nora was a person that Staci really didn't care for mostly because she was a pretender and too uppity when she was just a local project chick. Plus, Staci didn't like how Nora was always looking at Nocturnal like she might want to sample him. It wouldn't end well for her or any other chick, though. Yet, she dealt with Nora off the strength of Maisha.

Staci wobbled in and asked if the Campbell party had arrived and was told they had. She sucked her teeth at the revelation. She had wanted to arrive before them. She made her way to the booth where the two women had their backs to her discussing what they wanted to get into for the upcoming weekend. Rika was sitting on the opposite side with her head down and deeply engrossed into her cellphone.

"Hey, chicas!" she called out as she stuffed herself into the booth beside Rika.

"Hey, Staci, how are you doing?"

"I'm as well as can be expected, but I'm beyond ready to drop this load. I swear on everything I ain't poppin' no more babies outta me," she complained.

Maisha laughed loudly and rolled her eyes. "Girl, didn't you say the same thing about Sadie? You know you'll drop them as long as Noc wants them."

"I know, but I mean it this time. Right hand to the man, I'm not getting pregnant again."

"I don't blame you. I mean you have all these babies and you still haven't been upgraded to fiancée and definitely not wife. Shoot, you only getting older. I wouldn't keep destroying my body either. I mean what happens when he leaves you and you got stretch marks, three kids, and no college degree?" Nora asked.

"Whoa, that was unnecessary and harsh. Really, Nora? Why you read her like that?" Rika queried, finally glancing up from her phone, her eyes dancing between Staci and Nora.

Staci just stared at her bewildered by her attempt to throw shade. This girl had really come for her. Nora Jean was an attractive girl, but she was out of her league coming for Staci. Nora was about five-seven with a slim frame with no curvy hips. She had a small butt and a slim waist. She basically looked like a dark brown Michelle Williams from Destiny's Child, especially with her hair extensions. However, that slick tongue of hers was off putting, to say the least. If Staci wasn't pregnant and scared Nocturnal would beat her black and blue, she would have slapped the sass right out of this heffa. Instead, she chose to beat her with words. "This pregnancy brain has me forgetting everything. Exactly what title does your man have for you? I'll wait." A few seconds past then Staci spoke again, "Right, you don't have one so what are you classified as? Are you single, a side chick, or just wannabe gold digger? Nah, you're *nothing* because no man worth his salt would settle for you. Don't come for me *Nora Jean* because your armory will never defeat mine. I've been blasting trollops since summer of '08. Correction, I got a college degree, zero stretch marks, and will gladly rock my three children with pride. Boo, I'm the right one!" Staci clapped back.

"Well, then," Maisha commented, looking between Staci and Nora. The tension was thicker than old-fashion cheese grits. "Easy. I swear, Nora, next time I'm leaving you at home. Don't mind her, Staci. She's just in her emotions because Vicious got all in her feelings not once but *twice*. I told her to leave him alone. He's not the normal kind. I mean he's saved now, but that only means he won't kill you, not that he'll sugarcoat his words."

"That was funny. I told her Vicious don't play," Rika chimed in. "Staci, he kicked her out of the cookout celebration we had. She made the mistake of insulting him and cuzzo came out swinging. Even Grammy was laughing."

Staci lifted her brow at a now hushed Nora and smirked. "Vicious? Like of all the men to hit up, you chose to go for him? He's not even in your lane." Staci smirked.

"Really, y'all? I'm still sitting here." Nora sucked her teeth and rolled her eyes and neck. Whatever. He too broke for me anyway. I need somebody who can afford the finer stuff in life," she snapped.

"The devil is a lie. My cousin isn't broke. He might not know it, but I overhead my dad say he had a trust fund that he'll get access to when he's twenty-five, thanks to his other grandparents. His momma comes from money! Plus, he got a good job and is about to start college," Maisha corrected. "You're my girl, but Vicious is my blood and you ain't finna lie on his name or disrespect his character like that."

Well, that was news to Staci. However, she hadn't missed how Nora Jean's entire demeanor shifted like she was really going to get a piece of Vicious' money pie. "Nora, you're looking way too interested now. I hope you know Vicious don't do phony. He already knows whatchu about too, so he done put you on the list," she commented.

"Nor does he do *you*, boo. I didn't see you at the cookout. At Trek's, I didn't see him running up tryna converse with you. I heard he dissed you. Besides, I'on think he do black chicks no more. I saw him out with a white chick or maybe she was albino and her two kids playing family. Now, sip that tea. FYI, Staci, please believe when I put my mind to it, I can get any man I want." Nora sneered.

"Wait. What? Who was the girl?" Maisha and Rika asked perplexed.

"I don't know. I've never seen her in my life. I won't lie. She's a cute girl with fair skin. She's got a little body on her and has those colored eyes like Valor. The baby girl she had looks like Tamara Mowry-Housley's son, Aden, with that silky, bouncy, curly hair and blue-gray eyes. Vicious said she was his friend, but he came in carrying the older little girl who looked about six or seven. The toddler looked to be one or maybe younger. I'm sure it wasn't his baby, but they were the perfect picture of a cozy, little family."

"No, it's not his baby!" Staci quickly added, troubled. They all looked at her like she was bonkers. Maybe she was. Honestly, she couldn't see Vicious with anybody else and he told her back in the day, he didn't want children. Sure, he had been fifteen, but he was adamant about that, so now that he was released, he was dating chicks with kids and a white girl at that. She didn't like how that made her feel.

Maisha quickly pulled out her cellphone and dialed her cousin to find out who this mystery woman was and where he had met her. However, he never answered so she had to leave a message.

"Well, he ain't answering, but I'ma find out who she is. She hasn't visited my Grammy's house. We're getting to the bottom of this," Maisha vowed. Just when the words left her mouth, her cell started to ring.

"Is it him?" Staci queried way too thirsty, but she didn't care.

"Nah, this is my new friend."

"Oh, who is this friend and are y'all serious?" Staci nosily interrogated.

"She's seriously hiding their relationship, because even I don't know him. All I know is he's a white boy. She's in the swirl world," Nora interjected.

Maisha rolled her eyes and answered the phone and mouthed to the rest of them to hush. Staci turned her attention to Rika who was smiling as well. "Who you keep texting on that phone, girl?"

"Congo."

"What? When did this happen? I know your cousins don't know about it 'cause Trek, Vicious, and Val would be all in your business. Girl, are you still in high school? Y'all church girls sneaky and freaky. Word to the wise, let that grown man go because you're playing with fire."

"We just friends, so there ain't nothing to let go," Rika sassed.

Staci stretched her eyes but didn't speak on it. She just hoped that Rika knew what she was doing. These street dudes weren't nothing nice. Rika was a good girl. As far as she knew, Rika was still a virgin, and Congo wasn't the faithful and respectful type. Staci needed to dig deeper to see what was up. Even though she and Vicious weren't on good terms, she did love his family and did her best to stay connected.

Later that night...

Staci had just tucked the children in bed for the night and wobbled toward the kitchen. She was craving Graham Crackers and Gold Fish with Nutella spread. Just as she got her food, the front door opened and closed. She assumed it was Nocturnal and she was pissed at him. She really hoped he wasn't up to his deceitful ways again. He had cheated on her before with Lourdes, although he believed that Staci didn't know the identity of the female.

Staci told him flat out that there wouldn't be another cheating incident or he'd lose his family. But the fool had kept Lourdes around to manage his financial books. That was stress in and of itself. Like why keep her around? That was an issue. The other issue was she still had an empty finger but a full stomach. The statement that Nora had made was still fresh in her head and it really bothered her. If Noc wasn't going to marry her then she needed to pull out of the relationship and move on.

"Staci, where you at?"

Staci ignored him and took a bite out of her cracker. He eventually drifted into the kitchen, looking and smelling good. "Oh, so you didn't hear me calling you?"

"I heard you just fine, but since you ignored me and your kids today, I thought that was what we were doing."

Nocturnal grimaced at her. "Don't start that, Staci. I swear every time you get pregnant you get so deep in your feelings about every little thing. I wasn't ignoring you. I was working. Why is you whining like that? You sound worse than our kids."

Staci leaned her head to the side, staring at him like he'd lost his mind and placed her hands on her hip. Who was he speaking to like that? "Well, if you got an issue with how I act when I'm pregnant then stop knocking me up. In fact, I'll help us both. After this one, I'm getting my tubes tied. Don't make any sense for me be giving you babies when you can't give me a ring and a wedding. I ain't stupid. Let me find out you still messing around on me. I'll pull up and out of here so—"

She was interrupted by him hemming her up. "Say that foolishness again. Like you really trying to threaten me when you're the one who rolled up on *your* ex and didn't tell me nothing about it."

Staci pushed him off, not that he really moved, but he eased up his hold on her. "It wasn't like that. Maisha invited me to a party that Trek was throwing, and when I got there I saw Vicious and all I did was speak. Ask Congo. He was there. Unlike you, I'm faithful," she snapped.

"Nah, you opportunistic. Don't you recall how we started? You wanted a boss and was itching to get away from Vicious."

Staci rolled her eyes and pulled away from him. "I'm tired of this, Noc. If you don't want to marry me then the shop is closed. Every Sunday I go to church with my children feeling like I have a glowing scarlet letter. I want to get baptized and when I do, we won't be living in sin or fornicating. I just won't do it. I want better for our children. My daddy never married my mother. I got siblings all over South Carolina and beyond. I don't want that for Chauncory and Sadie," she cried and then sat back down on the chair and dropped her head for a moment to collect her thoughts. "You know I deserve better. I deserve a man who loves me enough to do right by me, and you don't, do you? You buy me stuff, but you don't really care about me. I wish I had never gotten pregnant again. We didn't even need another baby," she mused out loud.

"What's wrong witcha? You sound like a fool, you know dat? You don't have to work, you stay fly as do my children. I'm here for you and I ain't cheated since the last time. I'm even getting a house built for our family. You want to get married, and I do too, but can you let me finish transitioning from the streets? It takes time. I'm taking care of us and Penelope until her old man gets out. Then we can plan our future. You know I'ma marry you so why you're doing all this stressing and being extra is beyond me. Don't you ever say we don't need a baby," he fussed, letting out a hard breath. "All my kids are a blessing. I swear you want me to beat some sense into you. Your best bet is to eat them Gold Fish and take ya melodramatic butt to bed," he ordered and then turned to walk out of the kitchen.

"You must think I'm stupid. The same chick you cheated on me with is *Lourdes*. If you ain't messing wit her, then why she still maintaining your finances down in Atlanta?" she snapped angrily, clapping her hands as she spoke each word.

"Whatchu talkin' 'bout?"

"Not today, Noc. You can't even play me. You know what I'm talking about. I got my receipts and copies. You make me sick tryna keep secrets like I'm not a CIA investigator. I know about Congo and Rika and what's that about? Are you using her to get to Vicious? You just full of deception," Staci quipped, her eyes narrowed in fury.

"Whoa! Wait. Ain't nobody playing you. Who cares about the two of them? I don't need her for nothing. Don't come at me like that. Clearly, you're speaking on something you know nothing about," he replied, but she could tell that she'd hit a nerve.

"Really? Okay, so we're lying now? Cool." Staci nodded her head. "If Vicious finds out it's gonna get ugly. You know how he is about his family."

Nocturnal sighed and balled his fist. "Why are you worried? You low-key got feelings for Vicious? You having some lover's remorse and want him back, 'cause it ain't happening. You knew when you gave me my first son you had sealed your future. Don't force me to eliminate him. I have plans to utilize his talents. However, please note that I don't compete. I conquer, and you know you can catch it as soon as you give birth to my child. You know how I get down. You ain't the only insane one in this relationship."

"Whatever! I just better be getting a ring soon and you better do something about Lourdes, or I will. Because as you stated, we're both on the insane spectrum."

"Go to bed before I get annoyed and take off my belt and give you the butt whooping yo momma never did, Staci. You always doing the most. Ain't nobody cheating on you. I'm tired of hearing you sang that same line. How about you create the remix because this tune is getting old," he told her and left her standing in the kitchen.

Chapter 12

Grammy quietly entered the den and queried, "Why the long face, Theory?"

He smiled when he looked up and saw her standing there with a welcoming smile. "Grammy, Val and I were trying to find his twin, but Val doesn't remember her name and we really don't know where to start. Like do we contact a lawyer, the Department of Social Services or family court? Valor feels like she's in trouble, but without her name, how can we find her? I can't let him down, Grammy. Finding his sister is important to him, and I owe him that."

She offered him a warm smile. "That's what's the matter? I knew something was up between you two. Let me help. I know some people. Is that all?"

"What else is there?"

"A lot. You're doing well for yourself and I'm proud of how you've been working, going to church, and helping me. I also know you still carry pain from your past. I got something to tell you."

"Grammy, I don't like how you're looking. What is it?"

"Well, believe it or not, I heard from your father. He called and said he's working down there in New Orleans. He said he's clean and getting himself together. He heard from Walker that you were out. You know Clyde won't talk to him."

That was unexpected. Theory hadn't heard from Stanley Corrieon Campbell in decades. He wasn't sure how he felt about his Grammy speaking to him. He surely wasn't, but before he could reply, his cell vibrated. He inwardly thanked God for the interruption. It was a text from Virtuous and he couldn't hold back a grin. She pretty much texted him daily and called when her father wasn't around. He didn't like sneaking, but he understood her situation.

"Did you hear me about your dad? What's got you cheesing like that?" Grammy asked as she petted Logic.

"We can talk about your prodigal son later. Anyway, I met this girl a while back, and we had lunch not too long ago. Now, we just talk and text daily. She's cool, but her daddy is cray-cray. Like, she's seventeen, but never had a boyfriend or went on a date. I think she's like me."

"How so?"

"You remember on the news when they were talking about a mother beating one child and attempting to kidnap the other one?" he queried, and Grammy nodded. "That's her. Her moms abused her like my folks did me, or at least I surmised as much. She didn't like discussing it, but she had that same look in her eyes as I did when you got me. I just feel like we're kindred, but I'm taking it easy and being cautious. Her sisters like me too."

"She has sisters?"

"Yeah, two of them. They're younger and she takes care of them."

"What's her name?"

"Vivi and her sisters are Maddison and Tory. Hey, Grammy, I gotta get this. It's Archie."

"Okay." Theory knew she wanted to say more, mainly, about his father, which he was good on. That was a wound he wasn't ready to tamper with. Theory scooped up his dog and answered his phone. "Archie, what it is?"

"Bruh, do you have any plans this weekend?"

"On Friday night, I'm going to Val's game, but after that I'm open. Why?"

"You know that honey I met at Trek's party? Well, she wanted to hang, and I need a wingman 'cause she's bringing her girl from Atlanta. I hear her girl is bad, so Saturday night I need you."

"Bet, but let her girl know I ain't paying for nothing 'cause this ain't a date. I already got my eyes on a special one. I'm not jeopardizing my relationship with her for a favor to you."

"You's wrong. You can pay for her meal."

"If it ain't a McDonald's Happy Meal or Burger King's Big Kids Meal, I ain't paying because these millennial chicks a whole new breed. Their job is to seek and destroy. They for real on a devil mission and I refuse to get caught up. I'm hip to the game. You betta make it crystal clear for her to have zero expectations."

"Fine. I'll pay for her. Just be nice."

"I'll be *me*."

"You stupid."

"Well, you've been warned."

"Noted. I'll see you at Val's game tomorrow night then."

"Hold up. Why can't Shalamar do it?"

"Man, 'cause the girl ain't dark skin and too thin for his liking. Plus, he said he had a research paper due."

"Dang, a'ight, I gotcha. Tell her I'm Cinderella, so at midnight everything goes back to the default setting and I disappear."

Archie burst out laughing. "I swear you stupid, bruh. I'll tell her. One."

"One." Theory hung up and headed out. He needed to get in Maisha and Rika's business. Val had said that he thought Ri had a boyfriend, but it wasn't a boy at their high school. He was going to find out, especially since Maisha called herself getting in his business. Nobody but nosey Nora Jean had told them about Vivi, but that's cool. He had something for that motor mouth.

A & Ω

Virtuous let out a sigh. It had been a long day and Tory was fussy, but thankfully, she was asleep now. Virtuous had finished up her school work now and all she wanted to do was rest. Well, she wanted to rest and daydream about Theory. He made life so much more bearable. She flopped down on the couch and let out an overdue breath.

Soon, she'd be back with Greg and honestly, that was bothersome. She didn't want to return because she knew what going back to his house would do. Plus, she was giddy for the first time in her life about a guy. Theory excited her. He added to her happiness and he gave life new spice. They texted daily and each morning she sent him a Bible verse and he sent her a prayer. It was sweet. Even though they'd been friends for a short period of time, he had become the highlight of her day. She needed that. The Lord knew she needed something that was all her own.

Virtuous leaned down and picked up her sketch pad and started drawing her feelings.

"There you go. How is Tory feeling? LeAnn said she was fussy, and no one could calm her but her big sister," Cate commented.

Virtuous stopped drawing to give her attention to Cate who was now sitting on the edge of the recliner. She had a yoga and barre body. Aunt Cate was all about building her inner core. She was about five-feet-five with an A-line haircut, beautiful brown eyes, and naturally tanned skin.

"I just collapsed from fatigue. Tory is better. She and Maddison are knocked out. I just thought I'd sketch a little while it's quiet. Is Cary here?"

"No, he's out with his friends. Why aren't you out with Tamari? Don't you all have church tonight?"

"We do, but I won't leave Tory. Plus, Daddy doesn't like me to hang out with my friends outside of school."

Cate let out an exasperated sigh. "That annoys me how he acts like because Addison is gone that it's your place to be the *mom*. It's not fair to you. I also feel like because Addison has an opioid addiction that he thinks you will as well. It's so wrong. I was speaking to Norman about that the other day, and LeAnn and she agreed too. Hopefully, he'll ease up on you. It's your senior year in high school. You're supposed to have fun."

Virtuous just nodded her head in agreement, but she didn't vocalize her dismay with the situation. No one knew the real reason why Greg kept her so close. If she told them they wouldn't believe her. Her only hope was to graduate, get scholarships, and go to college far away. She wasn't applying to any South Carolina schools. She needed distance. She just had to hide it from Greg.

"Vivi, are you okay, honey? I notice sometimes when we talk, you kind of go to another place. I know it's hard to lose Addison, but I'm here if you need to talk about girl stuff. You can trust me."

No, she couldn't. At the end of the day, this was Greg's family. Virtuous didn't have a family. They were good to her, but that would all change when they discovered the monster that was Greg. "I'm just tired. I think I'll go to bed," Virtuous replied and quickly collected her items and jogged upstairs to prepare for bed.

After she showered, she grabbed her phone and called Theory. Just hearing his voice was soothing and helped her release tension.

"Hey, Proverbs."

She giggled. "Why do you call me that?"

"Because your name is Virtuous, and Proverbs 31 is all about the virtuous woman. Believe it or not, it was part of my Bible Study Wednesday night and all I thought about the entire time was you. You're going to get me in trouble with the Lord," he joked, which caused her to giggle harder. Once she stopped, he asked, "Whatchu doing? Is Tory feeling better?"

"I finally got her asleep and she is feeling better, but boy, am I drained."

"Good, I'm glad to hear she's better. You make sure that you take care of yourself or maybe you need to let me do that. So, when will I see you again?"

Holding her cheeks, she grinned giddily. She wanted to see him again too. She daydreamed about him most of the time. "Hopefully, Saturday. I've been approved to go to the movies and Ruby Tuesday so maybe we can meet then. I'd love for you to meet Tamari. She's my best friend."

"That's what's up. I'm down, just text me the time and location. I need to meet your peeps."

"I will. I'm sorry it's like this, but once I graduate, I'll have more freedom. Then I can see you whenever I want."

"Don't apologize, Vivi. I understand. You're busy with school and your sisters. Your dad depends on you and he's worried about you. Right now, I'm busy with work and trying to get into college, but it's working. We're taking it slow to see where this goes, so don't worry about it. I'm not going anywhere."

"Thanks. I wish I'd met you a few years ago. I like your chill. Like, you don't let anything get to you and I admire that," she confessed and was about to say more when she heard Greg's voice. "Theory, I gotta call it a night. Greg's here."

"A'ight, Proverbs, I'll hit you up later, but if things get out of hand, call me no matter the time."

"Okay, and the same goes for you. Goodnight, Theory." She hung up and deleted the thread on her phone just as Greg entered her room without knocking.

"Hey, are you okay? Cate said she was worried about you."

Virtuous wanted to roll her eyes. Cate didn't need to speak on her behalf to Greg. He'd just get paranoid and think she was up to no good. "I'm fine. I'm just tired because Tory's been fussy today."

"You sure?" he queried, closing and locking the door before sauntering over to her.

"I'm sure. Where's Jason?"

"He's got a girlfriend, so I had the conversation with him. I'm too young to be a granddad. I still want some more children," he told her as he massaged her stomach. He turned her around so that she was lying flat on her back and he straddled her. "Are you pregnant, Virtue?"

Virtuous glared at him like he'd lost his mind. "No. I'm not. I don't want to be," she replied.

"Why not? I want a son."

"You have one. I'm not missing out on my senior year, Greg. I have my hands full with Maddison, Tory, and my senior art exhibit."

"Calm down. I was just asking. We'll grow our family. If you want to wait a while, I guess that's fair. However, I'm don't like the way you talk back to me. This is your last warning. Don't piss me off, Virtue. I love you, but that don't mean I won't keep you in line."

"Yes, sir," she replied and then she tried to remove her body from his.

He leaned down and held her face stationary and kissed her hard. Then he got up, unlocked the door, and left. She closed her eyes and prayed. Every fiber in her body wanted to scream at the top of her lungs and tell because there was no way she was giving him another child.

Chapter 13

Theory, his two cousins, Maisha and Rika, and Archie were eating at Copper River Grill before heading to Valor's football game. Shalamar was invited, but he was working on his research paper. However, he promised to meet them at the stadium, which was cool because Theory wanted a small group since he needed to get talk to Maisha and Rika. He wanted to get all in their business, and this was the only way to do it and not be bothered with their other friend girls that he didn't care for.

"Get what y'all want," Theory told them after their waitress arrived. After their drink and food orders were taken, Theory got right to the business.

"Mai, what was up with that voice message you left me?" He turned slightly because she was sitting beside him.

"Oh, well, we were having lunch with Staci and—"

"Hold up. What y'all doing entertaining Staci? Your momma and daddy know you associate with her?"

"OMG, Theo, she's cool. Like, when you were arrested, she was devastated and came around a lot. Valor don't like her because you don't, but she's been like a big sister to me and Rika."

Theory sucked his teeth. "*OMG Mai*," he mocked. "I don't trust her. That's another conversation. What I want to know is who speaking on my name."

"Oh, that was Nora Jean. She said she saw you with a white girl and her children and that y'all were acting like a family. You got a girl and ain't told nobody?" Rika asked.

Theory shook his head. He really was starting to dislike Nora. How was she out in the streets making up stories about him? "I have a friend that I took out for lunch. Her grandmother had an emergency and she had to bring her sisters with her. No, she isn't white. She's biracial, but you know that means she's Black. Go tell nosey Nora to mind her business and to keep my name outta her mouth. She don't want what I'll bring."

"Say that again, bruh. She's an ole tricking, deceitful trollop. She thinks she's fly, but she be out here looking like day-old leftovers and smelling like an outdated Great Value spicy tuna fish pouch. Y'all need some new friends because y'all current crew is bringing down your dating value. Those females ain't trying to elevate themselves. They're just looking to be taken care of. Ri and Mai, y'all better than that. Befriend females that got goals, not ones trying to be gold diggers," Archie lectured.

"Preach it, Arch! Anyhow, Rika who has your attention? You're all in that phone," Theory commented doing his best not to laugh at Archie's dis of Nora.

"Oh, he's just a friend."

Archie gave her the side eye, which didn't go unnoticed by Theory. "Who is your friend?"

"Just a friend."

Getting frustrated, Theory turned his attention back to Maisha. "Mai, who is Rika's *friend*?" He'd noticed that when he was around Rika she was glued to her phone and when he inquired, everyone just stated it was what kids do these days, but he knew it was more than that.

That got Rika's attention and she stretched her eyes at Maisha in warning, but Theory wasn't having it. He could tell that Rika was hiding something and he wasn't about to let it slide. "Mai?"

"They're just friends, Theo."

"Hush," Rika pleaded.

"Who. Is. It?" Theory growled out. They were working his nerves.

"Congo," Maisha quickly spilled the beans after Theory turned dark eyes on her.

"What? You're talking 'bout King Kong Congo like the same one that's Nocturnal's do boy?" Archie queried, looking at Rika. Her entire face had paled, and her eyes were watering like she knew she was in trouble for real. "Congo is like a hundred years old. He's about to fossilize and you're barely ten. Girl, you're 'bout to get a butt beating for the ages. Even I'm mad and I don't get mad."

Maisha chuckled. "You're doing the most, Archie. It's more like twenty-five and sixteen."

"Rika Michelle Campbell, I know good and well your young tail ain't entertaining that grown man. He's way out of your league and you're way too good a girl for him. How did that even happen? I never let you meet Noc and his crew, so how?"

"Nah, Ri, don't start that sniffing now when two seconds ago you were grinning in that phone," Archie fussed.

Theory was about to go in when he heard a familiar voice. He looked over and saw a smiling Maddison. She was all decked out in red and black with a bulldog painted on one cheek and a paw on the other. He was sure that Vivi had painted it since she liked art.

"Hey, cutie," he cooed, getting out of his seat and bending down to her level. "Where's your sister?"

"I'm here." Theory looked up and smiled at Virtuous. She was decked out in school spirit too. She wore a fitted red Hilfiger polo dress and black converse shoes and she was holding Tory who had on the same designer, but her dress was black, and she wore red ribbons in her hair and red converse shoes.

"Hey. I thought I was going to see you tomorrow."

"Oh, are we interrupting?" she questioned, and he noticed that she was looking over at his cousins. Vivi didn't give off vibes of a jealous person, but he wanted to make sure that she didn't think he was that kind of man.

"No, not at all. Let me introduce you to my family." He told her, as he got up from his seat. He held out his hand and grasp hers. "Fam, this is Vivi, the beautiful young woman that Nora was talking about. These are her sisters, Tory and Maddison. Vivi, these are my cousins, Maisha and Rika. They're sisters. And this my best friend, Archie."

"It's nice to meet you all," she replied.

"Same here, shawty," Archie, retorted grinning.

"Y'all wanna sit with us?" Theory offered.

"I would, but we're here with my aunt and grandparents. Maddison saw you and ran off and I followed because I wasn't sure it was you. It's good to see you."

"Vivi, honey, our table is ready," LeAnn called out.

"Okay Mamaw, just give me a minute," she replied and then looked back at Theory. "I should go but hit me up later."

"Will do."

Then Virtuous did something that really surprised him. She gave him a hug and Maddison hugged his leg. "It was nice to meet everyone, and I hope I'll get to see you all again." Virtuous reached out for Maddison's hand and they sauntered off.

"Who is he?" Theory heard her grandma ask.

"He's a special friend."

"*Special?* Like, he's your boyfriend."

"No, Mamaw, he's *my* boyfriend," Maddison corrected.

Theory chuckled at cutie's correction.

"Mamaw, please!" Virtuous exclaimed, embarrassment laced in her tone.

"Well, I don't know what young people call it nowadays. He's handsome though. At least you have good taste, but we better not let your dad know or he'll have a conniption. Your Papaw started to wander over until I stopped him. I told him that you're beautiful so of course, young men take notice."

After that, Theory couldn't hear the conversation, but he was grinning all over himself. He'd take being a special friend.

"Dude, why are you smiling so hard?" Archie teased.

"Man, hush up. Now, back to what I was saying. Rika, you text Congo *now* and let him know y'all little relationship, situationship, or friendship is done. The only *ships* you need to be involved in are stewardship, fellowship, and discipleship with God. I'll be seeing Congo to make sure," Theory stated, switching up from cool and calm with Vivi, to vicious with his cousin.

She sucked her teeth in response.

"Keep sucking your teeth. Do it one more time and I swear you won't have them. Please believe I'm calling Unc. You think I'm playing if you want to, but I'm telling you Ri, you a church girl. You're not about that street life and you not built to be a street wife. Get it outta your head, and Mai, if you are following in Staci's footsteps 'cause you want a street king, I'ma get you too. You see what happened to me. It can happen to you too. Now, Rika, are you going to handle that or do I need to get involved?"

"No. I'll end it."

"Good. Now, see how easy that was?"

Archie chuckled. "Bruh, you're still vicious. I don't know why you won't let us call you that."

Just as Archie replied the waitress brought their orders and the group ate and chatted. As they got ready to leave, Theory caught Vivi's attention and waved her over. She said something to her family and got up to follow him. When she got close, he reached out to her and pulled her into a full hug. She felt so nice in his arms. He hadn't been with a woman since Staci but holding Vivi felt natural and right.

"So, I'm your *special friend*?" he muttered in her ear.

Virtuous pulled back and grinned. "You heard that?"

"Yeah, I believe you have some competition from your little sister. Cutie claimed me fast. I told you I'm a handsome dude. You got to be quick or you'll lose out," he teased.

Virtuous giggled. "Yeah, when it's just us girls, she talks about you. It's safe to say my sister likes you."

"What about you? Do *you* like me?"

"Theory, you know I like you." Her face flushed at her admission and he loved it.

"Vivi, when you blush like that does it affect your entire body?"

Her eyes widened in shock. "Theory!"

"I'm just messing with you. But does it?" Theory teased, making her grin harder. "Hey, I just wanted to see you before I left. My little bro is playing tonight so I gotta support him, but I couldn't leave without seeing you."

"I'm glad you did. We're headed to a game as well. My cousin plays football too."

"I'll call you tonight. Are you still going to be at your grandma's house?"

"Yes."

Theory nodded and pulled her into another hug and kissed her cheek. When he pulled away Virtuous had the dreamiest look in her eyes and offered him a sweet smile. "You like me."

"You like me too." Then she leaned in and kissed his cheek.

"Bye, Proverbs." Theory winked at her and she waved goodbye to him.

Chapter 14

Virtuous held Tory as the pair trotted up the steps to the bedroom. Virtuous needed to wash Tory and change her clothes. They'd had a great time at Cleveland Park and both girls had played until they couldn't anymore. Greg had suggested they come back to the house because Virtuous needed to get both girls ready. Mamaw was coming to pick them up. They were going to Greenville to Bon Secours Wellness Arena to see The Lion King musical production. Virtuous was a little upset she couldn't go because The Lion King was one of her favorite movies.

Once she got the girls dressed, they headed downstairs, and her grandparents were sitting in the den. They were still high off the Bulldog win. The boys had played excellent last night. Since everyone was so into the game, no one noticed when she'd ventured off to call Theory or at least she didn't think anyone had noticed.

"The girls are ready," Virtuous stated as Maddison zoomed past her and jumped on her grandfather.

"Greg, do you want us to bring the girls back tonight or just take them home with us?"

"Mom, let them spend the night, and I'll get them at church tomorrow. Jason's spending the night with one of his friends, so I think I'll hang with the guys tonight."

"That's good. You need a break after everything that has happened. Come on, girls, let's get going. Vivi, have fun on your outing." LeAnn winked before grabbing Tory.

"Girls, be good for Mamaw, but you can call me if you need me," Virtuous told them and she watched as they left. Greg stood behind her waving until they pulled off and then they both entered back into the house.

"What time are your friends coming over?"

"In like two hours."

Greg nodded. "You think you can cook me something before you start getting ready?"

"Okay. What do you want?"

"Just whatever."

Virtuous nodded and meandered into the kitchen with Greg right on his heels. "What about hamburger steak, loaded baked potato, and some veggies?"

"Sounds good to me, baby."

It annoyed her whenever he called her *baby*, but she didn't react. She just gathered what she needed while Greg planted himself on the barstool, gazing at her.

"You seemed really giddy yesterday," Greg mentioned.

"We won. I love Friday night football."

"Where were you going last night? I looked up in the stands and one moment, you were there and the next you were not. And then once the game ended, you got lost for a while."

Greg really did clock her movements. "I had to use the restroom. Did you see how much I was drinking? When the game was over, I went to congratulate the trio, Nimo, Cary, and Kasen," she replied as she turned on the oven and seasoned the hamburger. Greg didn't reply, and she went on about her business cooking.

With everything cooking, Virtuous rinsed her hands off and was preparing to exit the kitchen. Greg had been so quiet that she'd forgotten he was even present until he forced her body into his. The quickness of the movement startled her, but she did her best to remain calm.

"Greg..."

He turned her around and pushed her against the counter, effectively sandwiching her between it and his body. He was so close to her that what she exhaled, he inhaled and vice versa. "I know Nimo has a crush on you."

"That's just a rumor. He's never approached me in that manner and we're all just friends."

"You better be," he hissed.

She sighed loudly. She hated his repetitiveness about what she better or better not do. It was getting old.

"What's all that for?"

It was for being tired. "Can I ask you something?"

He leaned back. The nonverbal action was his way of saying yes.

"Why?" Virtuous questioned her soft voice barely audible, and her eyes full of doubt and insecurity. At the end of the day, all she wanted was a father, not an abuser or a lover, just a father. Why couldn't he just love her without hurting her?

"Why *what*, darling?" Greg queried. His wintery blue eyes gazed into hers as if the entire situation was normal.

"Why can't you be a dad to me like you are with your other three children?"

"I fell in love with you, Virtue. It wasn't done on purpose, but it happened. It's okay because you aren't my biological daughter. There's nothing wrong with us loving each other. Sometimes, stuff like that happens. You're my special girl and have been since you came to us. We've always had a unique bond."

Virtuous shivered at hearing that endearment. "But I'm your *daughter*, not your special girl. You and Addison are my legal guardians, and no, we don't share blood, but you're still my dad, the only father I've ever known. Why can't you love me without hurting me?" She was frustrated because he failed to comprehend her words and she was doing her best to fight back tears. Sucking up her sadness she controlled her emotion and tried another tactic. "How would you feel if someone did to Tory or Maddison what you do to me? If a man said the same things about your biological daughters would you feel the same way?"

Greg frowned, but she could tell that he didn't like the question, but he also didn't like the answer.

"Well?"

"I wouldn't let it happen, but that's not us."

"Greg, I'm someone's biological daughter. Can't we just be father and daughter? I need a father, not a lover," Virtuous implored and realized in that moment she should have stayed silent. He violently yoked her up scaring the life out of her. "Daddy, please."

"You're someone's daughter who didn't want you. Remember that!" he raged. "Is there someone else, Virtue? Why else would you be talking like this and acting ungrateful? Huh? You belong to *me*! Your body, heart, and soul are mine," he roared.

Virtuous was gasping for breath, but he was too strong and he was choking her. She slammed her fist down on his wrist to get his attention and to make him stop. He finally came to and then a look of desperation dressed his face, but not regret. "Virtue, baby, I'm sorry. You know I would never hurt you. I don't know what came over me," he expressed, banging his head with his hands.

Virtuous didn't reply because she was doing her best to breathe. She knew what had overcome him was his inner evil nature. He didn't love her. He loved to control her. She wanted to scream and fight. Her eyes looked at the pot of veggies cooking, and she thought about throwing it on him, but quickly let that idea go. Thankfully, common sense overrode her need for vengeance and she just walked away. It was time for her to get ready.

"Virtue?"

"I have to get dressed. My friends will be coming soon," she managed to speak.

A & Ω

The ride to the movie theater was quiet. Virtuous was deeply embedded in her thoughts. She was starting to feel like God had abandoned her. She'd text Theory, but she hadn't heard back from him, which was a blow to her heart. She was forced to wear a scarf to hide her bruises and her body ached. She was miserable and afraid.

When she got out of the shower, she saw the bruises on her back from a previous encounter and it saddened her more. Greg was really losing it. He had never been physically abusive to her like he'd been lately. She was at a complete lost as to what to do. She hadn't felt consumed by depression and suicidal thoughts in a while, but they were nipping at her now. It would be so easy to just give up.

"Vivi, are you okay?" Tamari asked, concerned.

Tamari had been asking her that ever since they'd picked her up. She couldn't tell Tamari the truth, though she felt like she was going to explode with all the secrets she was keeping. "Yeah, I'm just worried about my sisters. They haven't called me."

"You're such a mom. Mamaw has it all under control," Cary assured, shaking his head.

Virtuous nodded in agreement, but her facial expression didn't change. She knew the girls were safe, but she wasn't. Every part of her wanted Theory, but since he hadn't replied to her, she was concerned. If she lost him, if he was already done with her, it would be one more heartbreak that she wouldn't be able to sustain. His friendship was as necessary as air.

They arrived at the theater and everyone got out, all lost in their own conversations that Virtuous wasn't participating in. The group ambled up the concrete steps. Vivi's head was hanging down. She was uninterested in her surroundings. Cary held the door and she entered deeply in her thought and downcast.

"Aye, what I tell you about holding your head down?" a familiar deep baritone boomed.

Virtuous' head shot up and a smile instantly graced her face when saw Theory. He was there with the same two girls he'd introduced her to at the restaurant. Now that she was able to get a good look at them, she realized they all favored. Completely forgetting her friends, she trotted over to him and hugged him. "You didn't text me back." It sounded desperate even to her own ears, but she didn't care. She lived for his texts, conversations, and attention because it allowed normalcy in her life. Additionally, he never made her feel used or unworthy. He was always there to uplift and inspire, making her feel human and real whereas Greg made her feel like trash.

"That's why you're looking somber? You thought I wasn't coming? I'm sorry, Proverbs. I left my phone at my house. There's no way I'd miss an opportunity to spend time with you."

Virtuous nodded gleefully and pulled back, but before she could recover, her scarf unraveled from her neck, displaying her bruises. She tried to hide them, but the look in Theory's eyes let her know he'd seen them. Everything in her wanted to disappear. She was so ashamed.

"Don't," Theory told her and reached out and brought her quaking body into him. He held Virtuous protectively and she let out a comforting sigh. Virtuous knew what he was referring to. He didn't want her to drop her head in shame. He never wanted her to hide from him.

"Vivi, you've been keeping secrets. Who is this fineness?" Tamari queried, checking Theory out with a smile on her face.

He didn't even let Virtuous speak. He took control, allowing her to rest in his embrace. "Hey. I'm Theory. If you don't mind, I'ma take Vivi with me. I left my cell at home and she's going to ride with me to get it. We'll be back. These two ladies are my cousins, Maisha and Rika. They're going to stay," he decreed in a manner that brooked no argument.

Virtuous glanced around and saw the that the guys were flummoxed, but they remained silent. The way that Theory held her gave off the vibe that they were together, so maybe that was why the guys were in various stages of silent surprise.

"Oh, okay," Tamari replied before turning to the guys and introducing Theory's cousins and explaining the situation. "Guys, this is Vivi's boo, and she's going with him to get his phone. They'll be back," Tamari announced, and Theory smiled.

Then Tamari turned to Virtuous and mouthed, "You owe me an explanation." Virtuous shook her head in agreement.

"I appreciate that, Tamari," Theory replied. He reached out for Vivi's hand and escorted her out of the movie theater to his truck. He opened the door for her and she got in, doing her best to hide the tears that fought to fall.

"Who hurt you?"

Virtuous shook her head, not wanting to tell him because she knew he couldn't do anything about the abuse she was suffering. She desperately needed to seek solace in her *World of All*.

"A'ight." Then she watched as he padded around his truck and get into the driver's side and they pulled off. He had an indecipherable facial expression, so she couldn't tell if he was angry or not. His chiseled features weren't tense, and there was no fury lingering in his eyes. No, the only action that exhibited any emotion was the killer grip he had on the steering wheel. However, she remained silent as the sounds of Christian rapper Tedashii filled the speakers. She just nodded her head to the music just to do something to soothe her nerves.

"You know this dude?" he asked, his tone just as cryptic as his facial expression.

"Yes, I only listen to Christian rap. Well, I like Drake too, but I only have the clean versions of his music. I'm really into Alessia Cara too. Her album is so poetic."

"My Grammy don't play that secular music either. No devil music in her house. Those are *her* words and not mine. If the lyrics disrespect women, Val and I can't play it. He's the one who got me on these Christian rappers. Lecrae, KB, Flame, and116 are my favorites so far, though."

"I like them too. I think you'd really like NF also. His music is so real, raw, and honest that I just gravitate to it. He knows pain. That album Therapy Session is my joint."

"Well, then I have to cop that. I haven't had my iPhone that long, so I need some suggestions for my music library."

"Really? Where have you been?"

"If I tell you, then you have to tell, me who hurt you," he countered.

Virtuous chewed on her top lip while she mulled over his words. She did want to tell someone. That's all she'd ever wanted to do, but fear of not being believed had made her stay silent and suffer. "Okay."

"For the past six years, I was locked up. I robbed somebody and got caught." She saw him out of her peripheral vision. She could tell he was waiting for her to react. She wasn't judgmental because there were people who attended their church who had done jail time. "As long as your name isn't on the sex offender's registry and you don't have DV charges, then you're all good with me."

He let out a breath. "Nah, I don't get down like that. But you aren't concerned that I was locked up?"

"No, we all make mistakes. As a Christian, what right do I have to judge another of God's children? You did your time and I assume you aren't seeking to break the law again. Plus, you were young, a teenager. And according to my psychology teacher, your brain is still developing. I don't view you differently if that's what you're wondering. Besides, I see *you*, Theory. You've been kind to me since we first met. My little sister thinks the world of you and when I'm around you, you have this ability to make me feel seen. I feel protected and connected to you in a way I've never felt with anyone else. It is easy with you, conversation, being silly, and sharing my space. So, no, your past is just that, and I feel no need to attack you for something you've paid for."

Theory smiled. "Girl, you're older than seventeen." He paused before continuing, "I knew you were feeling me," he replied and took his hand and ran it down her cheek. "So, who hurt you, Vivi? I need to know. Somebody put hands on you and that means I'm doing the same to someone. I know we're taking it slow, but I care about you and I want you safe."

"It was an accident."

"Nah, Virtuous, I didn't ask for the preface nor do you need to lie to me. Just tell me the truth, let me know who hit you."

"My dad."

A & Ω

Everything in Theory's body tensed. He had seen her father and knew just how much larger he was than her. Theory and Virtuous spoke daily either via text or cellphone. She was sweet like pure cane sugar and there was nothing she could have done that would have justified the marks he saw on her neck. The reason he was so attracted to Vivi was because of her affectionate and sweet personality.

Theory wanted to annihilate her dad. *How dare he hurt his Vivi?* From the first day that Theory had seen her in Gaffney, he knew she was someone different, but he never thought her father was beating her. However, this discovery explained her reaction to him upon their first and second meetings. She was really terrified of her father, and he knew that fear. He had felt it too from his own parents.

Pain recognized pain and Vivi was in horrific pain and probably felt isolated and as if no one cared or wanted to help her. That had been him so many times. His soul had called out for help, but he'd found no relief until Grammy and now, he needed to be a beacon of light and deliverance to her. God had brought her to him for a reason, and he wasn't going to fail God or Virtuous.

Theory let out a calming breath because he didn't want to add to her anxiousness. It was obvious that she was upset. "Is that the only marks you have?" He couldn't believe her father had choked her, and he knew if that had happened, then his abuse was escalating, and the result could be death. This wouldn't end well for Virtuous. She needed to get out.

"Theory..." Her voice sounded full of anguish torture. He didn't like that sound. He liked the melodious humming that calmed him instantly, not the fear and hurt. He closed his eyes again just to quiet the violent voice inside of him. He wanted revenge. He wanted to serve Virtuous' father the same beating he'd inflicted upon her. He wasn't Vicious anymore. He was Theory, a saved child of God, he mentally chanted.

"Tell me, Vivi. I need to know. I want to know *everything* so I can help you. Does your dad beat on your sisters too?"

"No, they're his biological children. He's just my legal guardian."

"So, your parents beat you because you're not their biological child?" he questioned incredulously. She was their child if they had legal custody.

Silence.

Theory turned to her when they stopped at a red light. She was crying. Her body was trembling, her skin was red, and she was fiddling with her hands. "Vivi, you can tell me. You can trust me. Tell me what's happening," he coaxed.

"You won't like me anymore."

The light turned green and Theory drove, but then pulled over to the shoulder of the road. He extended his arm out and rested his hand on her shoulder slowly, caressing her to help her relax. "I swear that nothing you say will change how I feel about you. Sorry, but as corny as this may sound, you've bled into my heart and imprinted my mind, Vivi. You're basically stuck with me. You know my past and you didn't judge me, and in return, I refuse to judge you," he vowed.

She let out a hard breath. "I have a baby. Tory, is not my sister. She's my *daughter*."

That was a shock. The thought had crossed his mind, but when she acted so shy around him and informed him that she never had a boyfriend, the thought went away. "Wait. So, your dad is Tory's dad too?"

"Yes. The reason Addison attacked me was that she was tired of Greg using me for his pleasure. He said it's okay because he's in love with me and I'm not really his daughter. It's been happening since my thirteenth birthday."

Theory snapped and slammed his hand into the steering wheel. "Since you were thirteen?! He's been raping you for four freaking years and your mom never did anything to stop it? Virtuous, I'm so sorry," he told her and unbuckled her seatbelt to pull her closer to him. He wasn't sending her back to the lion's den. "You're not going back to him. That's physical abuse and *rape*! He won't ever touch you again."

"I gotta go back. I can't leave Tory with him. She's with her grandparents and will stay the night with them, but I don't like to leave my baby alone or my sister."

Theory broke out in a cold sweat. He kept running his hands over his face, but he was legit pissed. He cared about Virtuous. This girl had him acting out of sorts, wanting to watch rom-com movies, listen to pop music, and entertain her sisters. Now, he was ready to kill for her safety. He was willing to go to prison for her. Had he been in Vicious mode her pops would have been popped by now, but he was a saved man now, not a savage. God, this kind of wickedness threatened to pull him back into the darkness that his grandmother had prayed him out of. His body started to quiver with anger and then he felt her small hand on his shoulder.

"How do your grandparents not know?"

"My daughter passes for white. She has Greg's eyes and my skin is so fair. I believe one of my biological parents is white. Also, once I started to show, they took me out of school. At the time, Addison thought she was pregnant too, so they just passed Tory off as their child."

He shook his head in disbelief. "What kinda people are they?" he fumed.

"I'm sorry. I shouldn't have told you. I didn't mean to tick you off. It's just that it's so hopeless. I've kept it secret for so long that sometimes, I think I won't survive to see another day."

"Don't apologize. I'm glad you told me. It's not hopeless. I'll protect you, your daughter, and cutie too. It's not your fault, Proverbs. He's wrong and *sick*. No one deserves to be treated that way. We can go to the police. Even though I don't care for cops, I'll do it for you."

"It won't work. I can't because *he's* a cop, Theory," she cried out and pulled him tighter. "He's the resource officer at my school. I can't escape him. He's everywhere. Even if I told my story, no one will ever believe me over him."

"I believe you," he told her and kissed her forehead. "I believe you and I'll find a way to help you." Why did this fool have to be a cop? Virtuous was right. The code of blue was real, and they rarely turned on their own. Even though his juvie record was sealed, if her father found out about him, what would he do to Proverbs?

Chapter 15

Theory really didn't want to go out because he was too worried about Virtuous, but she had promised him that she was going to stay with her grandparents and Greg had gone out with his police buddies. Theory was so concerned about her after her confession, so he'd held her a little longer and let her cry it all out.

They had bonded. She had become an extension of him, and he wasn't going to permit anyone to hurt her. He'd held her in his arms until the truck's windows steamed up and then he drove to his house to grab his phone. Then they'd headed back, but Vivi hadn't wanted to watch the movie. She just wanted to be with him. She'd told him she wanted to have good memories, so they had wandered around the shopping center, held hands, made jokes, and talked about the future until the movie ended. Then the group went to eat. Virtuous was really shining during that time and it brightened him up also. His cousins liked her instantly. It was like they were all friends. He even liked her cousin, Cary, and his two friends. They'd reminded him of Val.

So, here he was with Archie as they headed out to pick up Yulonda, Archie's girl, and her friend, Lourdes.

They arrived at the apartment complex and Archie got out. "Bruh, are you coming in?"

"Nah, I gotta check on Vivi."

"A'ight, I'll be right back."

Theory nodded and called Vivi.

"Hey, you! I'm okay. The girls and I popped some popcorn and we're watching Disney cartoons."

"Has he tried to contact you?"

"He called to check on us, but he's not coming over. He's drunk."

"What about your brother?"

"As far as I know, he's spending the night elsewhere. Just to let you know, my brother has never touched me like that."

He let out a relieved sigh. "I miss you. I wish I could've brought you and the girls to my house."

"I miss you more. I wish we could've spent the entire day together. I wish it were all different."

He wished the same. "Our time is coming. I promise you that." He was going to say more, but he heard Tory getting fussy and cutie talking, so he knew it was time to cut it short. "Vivi, call me if you need me."

"I will. I promise, and Theory, thank you."

"Anytime, sweetness, good night." He could hear her smile and that relieved him.

"Good night."

Just as he hung up, the girls approached the car. He got out of the front seat and headed to the back without giving them much thought. His mind was on three little ladies, not these chicks.

"Okay, I see you," the girl commented, sucking on a lollipop and giving him a flirtatious smile.

It was wasted. He didn't even reply. He just got in the back seat and shut the door. This girl wasn't his type.

"Well, he's rude. He better be glad I like 'em like that."

"Lourdes, you're a mess," Yulonda teased.

Lourdes shrugged her shoulders and walked around and got in on the other side. Girl was stacked. Her legs were a mile long, he noticed as she entered the car. She had a nasal septum piercing and when she licked out her tongue, he saw her piercing there also. She was one of those females used to being the center of attention and thought all men wanted her. That vibe was coming loud and clear.

"You like what you see?" she asked.

"I'm Ray Charles, so I don't see nothing. Besides, I got somebody. I'm just doing my boy a favor."

"Well, a'ight then. I'm not trying to get a ring or nothing. I'm beautiful boo. I'm doing *you* a favor."

"If you say so," Theory replied and turned his attention back to his phone.

Lourdes burst into laughter. "Boy, you're really rude. I'on know what's wrong with you country boys. Well, where your girl at?"

"That's not any of your concern. Don't ask me about her. We don't need to even converse."

"Don't mind him, Lourdes, he's just in rare form today," Archie interjected, shaking his head.

"It's whatever. I got thick skin."

They continued the ride with Theory being engrossed in his phone, texting Vivi and Val. Val had been busy between sports, his job, and academics, so they'd hardly seen each other lately. He missed his little bro.

Twenty-three minutes later, they pulled up at a little upscale spot in Anderson. It seemed Archie was trying to show out for his woman. Yulonda did seem cool. She spoke in clear concise sentences, she didn't curse when she spoke, and she didn't address her home girl with derogatory slurs that many young and some older women did. That was something he'd noticed as soon as he got released.

Women didn't hesitate to call each other a female dog or garden tool. He couldn't comprehend why that was acceptable. In this day in age, a woman who had respect for herself and others was like seeing Big Foot, but Yulonda seemed to be legit and worth impressing. He wished his boy well. She might be a keeper.

As the group made its way to the entrance, Theory glanced over at Lourdes. She had on five-inch red heels, a mini skirt, and a crop top. She was not properly dressed for where they were going. If that was how she wanted to rock, then so be it. "Did my boy tell you about midnight? I'm going to disappear on you for real," Theory reiterated.

Lourdes laughed, showcasing the thin gap between her upper teeth. Her eyes sparkled like she really thought he was a comedian or something. Theory was serious, though. He already felt guilty about being in Anderson and not in Boiling Springs where Vivi was. They weren't officially together, but his heart was pretty much set on her. This situation felt wrong. "I like you, Theory. I appreciate you keeping it real with me. You're refreshing."

Theory nodded and held the door open for her.

Once they were seated, they all had a little small talk and he found out a wealth of information. Yulonda was attending Anderson University and was a political science major, working part time at a law firm, which Theory liked because the girl had goals. She was somebody he could see Maisha befriending. Lourdes was a finance and business administration major at Clark Atlanta University. Once Theory put his phone down, he found he enjoyed their company, but his mind was still on Vivi. He was trying to figure out a way to get her and the girls away from their sick father. The entire situation upset him.

"Theo, you're cool man?"

"Yeah. Sorry my mind wandered."

"If it's about Vivi, you know she'll call you. If nothing else, I could tell on Friday the girl is legit feeling you. Even her little sisters like you," Archie replied.

"I appreciate that, bruh." Theory attempted to shake off the feeling. He knew she would call him if she needed him, even cutie, knew how to use Vivi's phone to call him. Still, there was prickling tension that ran rampant throughout his body, and he couldn't identify why, but if anything happened to Vivi or the, girls he would lose it.

When he looked up again, the waitress was bringing their food. Once everyone had been served, Theory blessed their meals and began to eat. The conversation was limited as they ate, and all agreed that they didn't want dessert. And even though Theory had said he wouldn't pay, he did take care of the bill for himself and Lourdes. He really wanted to get back home to check on Virtuous. He wished that Val had met her already because his little bro could do a welfare check on her.

"What y'all doing here?"

Theory pivoted because he knew that voice and hoped to God, he never had to hear it again, but every time he visited Anderson, he risked the chance of running into her. There Staci was with Nocturnal, and his boy, Congo, and it looked like Nora Jean. Why was that chick everywhere like a fly?

"Leaving," Theory answered. This was the first time he had physically seen Nocturnal, and not much had changed. He still had that hood swagger about him that once seemed alluring to Theory, but now, it was just annoying.

"Hol' up," Nocturnal called out, looking from Theory to Lourdes. Theory could tell the wheels were turning in his head, but he wasn't sure why. "Lo, whatchu doing wit him and why are you here and not Atlanta?" he queried as he pulled up his bagging jeans, which was the universal sign for squaring up. That tickled Theory because Nocturnal couldn't beat him even if Congo tried to help.

"I'm visiting my people. Yulonda is my family, not that it's any of your concern."

"The *question is* Noc, why are you concerned about her movements. I'm right here pregnant with your child and you really questioning this female 'cause she with another man?" Staci fumed.

"My name is Lourdes, not female, female."

181

"This probably won't end well, but for the sake of arguing, both of y'all are females, so..." Archie mumbled as Yulonda pulled Lourdes back to calm the escalating argument.

Right then and there, Theory got the entire situation. Lourdes must have messed around with Noc previously or currently. Staci had found out about it, which would explain the extra attitude and why she was temporarily suffering from Tourette's syndrome. Her face and mouth were twitching and shaking. Interesting... *The way you get 'em is the way you lose 'em*, he thought to himself. The Bible states that you reap what you sow, and Staci was just getting her due.

Nocturnal ignored Staci and kept his eyes firmly on Lourdes and Theory, which clearly incensed and irritated Staci. "Lo, come speak to me for a moment." Noc requested. Theory just shook his head. This wasn't a good look. It was one of those moments when he was ashamed to be the same race as those around him. They were really acting stereotypically.

"I'm good. You said to only contact you when it's about business. I have no business to discuss. Don't be rude in front of my date," Lo fussed.

Lourdes was misinformed because this wasn't a date. "Aye correction, this ain't a date. You're not my girl, so if you and Noc got unfinished business to discuss, then do your thing, Ma." Then Theory looked over at Congo and narrowed his eyes. Now, they had business. He better stay away from Rika and stay with Nora's fraud self.

"We got a problem, Vicious?" Congo asked with a knowing glint in his eyes that irritated Theory.

"That depends on you, Congo. If you've stopped entertaining Rika, then we have no problem, but the moment you start, yeah we'll have a serious problem."

Congo chuckled. "Chill, young buck. She too young for me, but when she hit eighteen—"

"Nah, not even when she hit thirty, ol' head. You got the right one now. Keep them foul frauds on your arm because my cousin isn't for you. Oh, and Nocturnal, Trek told me you were looking for me for a business venture, but don't waste your time. I'm forever unavailable." Then he nodded to Archie. "Archie, let's be out. We're making the good white folks uncomfortable and when that happens, police get called. I can't catch a charge or a bullet."

Archie nodded in understanding and grabbed Yulonda's hand. They began to make their exodus while other patrons gawked at them. Staci's shrill voice was going in on Nocturnal, causing the group to chortle. Once they got back to the car, Theory had to ask, "Lourdes, Noc sent you to butter me up so I'd accept his proposal."

Lourdes had a confused look on her face and shook her head in the negative. "No. We got history, but he broke it off when his girl left him and took their kids. I tried to rekindle the flame, but he shut me down. So, I don't know what his little tantrum was about."

"You work for him?" Theory interrogated.

"Now you want to talk to me? Yeah, I do. I'm his bookkeeper."

Theory digested her words, quickly deciding to be done with her. Anyone associated with Nocturnal was a snake. He knew Nora Jean and Staci were snakes. The only theory, and no pun intended, that he could come up with was that Nocturnal thought Lourdes was plotting against him, but that was far from the truth. Theory hadn't sought revenge on Nocturnal because dude wasn't worth it, and he had nothing that Theory wanted. Shaking the thought, Theory discontinued the conversation and reached out to Rika to let her know she better stay away from Congo and get some new friends. He didn't want his cousins around Staci, Nora or the rainbow twins.

A & Ω

Staci was so hot that she'd ordered a Lyft to come pick her up. The entire time that Nocturnal spoke to that female, her blood pressure rose. Then to see Lourdes with Theory just sent her into a delirious fury. Her vision became blurry, she had a hard time hearing over the thumping of her pulse, and she felt dizzy.

How had that tramp gotten not one but two of her men? Then the way that Nocturnal dismissed her when he saw Lourdes was like he was really upset about her being out with a new dude. Hot tears spilled down her face followed by sharp pains surging through her abdomen that nearly brought her to her knees. She pushed on. She could fall apart in private. She caressed her stomach to assuage the cramps. It was not working and all she could think about was the doctor telling her she needed to avoid stress, or she'd be on bed rest. She wasn't even seven months yet.

"Staci, baby, calm down. Come back here, Staci!" Nocturnal requested.

"Don't speak to me and don't touch me. I swear I'll taser you back to the Creator. I'm done. I told you if you disrespected me it would be over. Boy, did you disrespect me!" she fussed and then her Lyft arrived. She painfully ambled over to it with Nocturnal right behind her. "Leave me alone or so help me God your momma going to be suit shopping and casket picking!" she quipped as she opened the back door to get in.

Nocturnal did as she'd demanded. Staci shut the door in his face and then gave him the one figure salute. "Ma'am, can you take me to the hospital? Something is wrong with my baby."

The driver's eyes widened, but she took off, leaving Nocturnal in the parking lot. As soon as they were on the road, Staci phoned her mother and asked her to bring her children to the hospital. She grabbed her stomach and prayed her baby would be safe. She would never forgive Nocturnal if she lost her baby.

"Ma'am, you should calm down. Stress isn't good for your baby."

"I know. I'm trying," she replied, and her phone started ringing. It was Noc, but she wasn't answering. Staci sent him straight to voicemail. He thought he could just hurt her and then pull her back in at his convenience. Well, she wasn't that thirsty. She had something for him. She had news that would cut him so deep and if he didn't get right she was about to get so wrong. Payback was coming for him. She put that on everything.

Chapter 16

irtuous woke to the hungry cries of Tory. She quickly jumped out of bed to quiet her because she didn't want her to wake up Maddison who was now curled in a ball holding her Doc McStuffins doll. She leaned over and kissed Maddison before picking up Tory. *How could any parent, foster, legal guardian or biological, ever hurt an innocent child? How could God, knowing the stories of His children before they were even born, allow men like Greg and women like Addison to have children?* That's what she couldn't reconcile and why her conversations, prayers, and Bible studying were decreasing. It was just too hard to ask God for help when He had allowed her to suffer for so long.

Removing the thoughts as Tory's cries increased, Virtuous made her way out of the bedroom and down the stairs to the kitchen. To appease Tory, she gave her an organic soft cookie while she warmed goat milk and got cereal. She put it all inside Tory's sippy cup. Once they got settled at the kitchen table, Virtuous hummed a lullaby as Tory suckle the nutrients in her sippy cup.

"Is that good, baby girl?" Virtuous cooed, tickling her daughter's cheek. She could tell that Tory was getting sleepy, so she put the empty sippy cup in the sink and then her Spidey senses tingled. Like for the first time, she noticed that they weren't alone.

"Virtue," Greg's voice slurred. "I'm hungry."

The stench of alcohol filtered through the air, causing her stomach to roll as a buried memory surged through her mind. She closed her eyes to relax the increase beating of her heart. When he was like this, he was terrifying.

How had she been so stupid? Her cellphone was upstairs in the bedroom and she was stuck here with her baby and Greg. Keeping her daughter in her arms, she headed toward the fridge and removed the deer meat that Mamaw had cooked and retrieved wheat bread from the bread box. Then she began to assemble his sandwich. Just like Maddison, he didn't like the crust on his bread, so she removed it and then cut the sandwich in half with a side of mustard and sat the plate in front of him. He also requested some warm milk, which she made somberly and ever so quietly. When he was drunk anything could set him off. She just wanted to make it out of the kitchen unmolested.

Virtuous sat down his milk and with a now sleeping Tory, she sought to make a quick escape and get back to her room, lock the door, put a chair under the doorknob and sleep. Her plan failed, though. As she attempted to leave, Greg reached out his arm, latched onto her waist, and pulled her back, apparently sober enough to be stronger than her. "Sit down with me. I hate to eat alone."

Virtuous tried to wiggle out of his reach and grabbed a chair, but he tugged her while she was holding Tory, bringing her down to his lap. "How was your day? You had fun with Cary and Tamari?" he queried as if this interaction was normal.

"I did." She saw him nod as he took a bite of his sandwich with his left hand while his right held her securely in place. Greg sat his sandwich down and then turned her into him. He placed his hand on the column of her throat, she instantly gasped, assuming he would choke her again. But instead, he just caressed the bruised spots. A sorrowful expression displayed on his face. She did her best not to recoil, but her neck was still sensitive and she had kept it hidden all day. "Baby, I'm sorry. I should've never put hands on you. I tried to drink the memory away. You know I love you, right?" She nodded her head, knowing that was what he needed to see. "Good baby. I'm crazy for you. Don't ever forget that. When the divorce is final with Addison, everything will go back to normal. I'll make it up to you. I won't touch you like that again. I swear."

"Okay, but I need to get Tory back to bed." She didn't believe his lies.

"Let me finish my sandwich and we can all go together. I missed you, Virtue."

After the request left his month she hardened. Theory would be so pissed if he knew she was even sitting on Greg's lap, but to share a bed again was out of the question. Now that Theory knew the truth about her predicament, it felt immoral. She attempted to shimmy free, but his grip just strengthened, and she felt the fight slowly diminished until she heard another pair of footfalls. Greg heard them too, but his intoxicated brain was slow to respond.

"Daddy, are you here?" Jason called out, shocking Virtuous. She didn't even know that Jason had come to their grandparents' house. She thought he was staying with a friend. Thank God for that blessing. Maybe God still heard her.

"Jay, that's you?"

"Yeah, Daddy, it's me," Jason replied as he entered the kitchen. Virtuous observed him take in the scene. His eyes were sympathetic and warming. He gave her a look like he was going to help her. "Vivi, you and Tory should go to bed. I believe I heard Maddison calling out for you. I'll stay with Daddy while you take care of the girls," he suggested and then proceeded to remove her from Greg's tight grasp.

"Jay, what're you doing? Virtue and I were having a moment. Now, go to your room."

"I'm helping my sisters. Besides, I wanted to talk to you about stuff," he added and then turned to Virtuous and mouthed, "*Go.*"

Virtuous didn't even stop to analyze what had just transpired. She took off like a bullet, shooting to her bedroom. Once there, she locked the door and put a chair under the doorknob. After that, her attention went to Maddison who hadn't moved an inch. She then placed Tory down and reached for her cell. She was going to send Jason a short thank-you text but stopped when she saw she had several missed calls from Theory and a few text messages.

She quickly called him back. Hearing his voice did wonders for her soul. His melodious voice soothed her instantly.

A & Ω

Staci knew something was wrong with her baby. She was just twenty-eight weeks, which was too early to give birth, but the cramping had worsened while the driver drove her to the hospital. Her child was coming, and her anger had turned into anxious fear and tears cascaded down her face, ruining her stoic façade. She loved Nocturnal, but he had shown his true colors and she was done with him. She could no longer hold on to what wasn't there. If he wanted a woman like Lo, he could have her. All she wanted now was for her baby to be okay.

Her words came back to her, and she felt so much guilt. She was the one who had said they didn't need another baby, but God, she wanted her child. No matter what, the baby was a part of her and if she lost her child, she would lose her mind. She started to pray, imploring God to save her child and to ease the pain she was feeling. She told God if He let her and her child survive, she'd leave Nocturnal and raise her children right.

"Please, Jesus, don't take my baby," she chanted, rocking back and forth until she arrived at the hospital. Everything was a blur and she barely remembered her name because the pain had become so intense. She just prayed and then calmness came over her.

A & Ω

Nocturnal glanced over at Congo who seemed to be in better spirits than him, but the dude was single, so he didn't have to deal with messy females. Nocturnal felt deflated and defeated. He'd reacted badly when he saw Lo with Vicious. He owned that, but how could Staci just leave? She not only left, but she'd ignored all his phone calls until she just turned the phone off. He was so pissed.

"Noc, bruh, you were wrong. You disrespected your wifey. The mother of your lineage and legacy, who is currently pregnant with your third, for a female you supposedly ain't rocking wit."

He shook his head because he knew Con was right. "I know. It wasn't even like that. I just saw her with Vicious and thought they might've been plotting against me."

"That's why I told you not to mess with that chick. Use her for her talents, but you didn't have to sleep with her knowing she had knowledge of your operation. Now, you're paranoid. So, what we gon' do?" he queried. "Honestly, I don't think Vicious cares about your businesses. He was never dealer material."

"Nah, but he's a leader and he's intelligent. Therefore, he's a threat. Who's to say he's not on some revenge tip to get back at me? I took his girl, knocked her up three times, and now, he's taking my side chick? Well, she's my old side chick," he corrected.

"Nah, he said they weren't dating, and I believe him. Dude's a lot of things, but he's honest. Even though I didn't appreciate his attitude, I think he's legit. I get it. You think they want payback, but I don't think Vicious cares. He didn't give Staci a glance. Plus, he had half a decade to deal with it. Now, what you need to do is find Staci and work this out."

He nodded in agreement and then his phone rang. "Hello?"

"Percy..." Nobody but Staci's mom, Sharifa, addressed him as Percy.

"Yes, ma'am?"

"Staci's in labor. She's having the baby. Since it's so early, they are more than likely going to have to airlift the baby to Atlanta's Children's Hospital. Whatever happened tonight caused her to go into premature labor. She don't want you here, but I told her you had a right to see your child."

"Wait. She's only six and a half months pregnant. The baby ain't even done developing."

"I know that, Percy, hence the reason I said *premature*. Boy, this is not the time to be dumb!" she shouted, causing him to ball up his face. If she wasn't Staci's mom, he would have cursed her out for that disrespect.

"A'ight, we're coming." He ended the call then looked at his friend. "Con, we gotta go. Staci's in labor."

A & Ω

A few hours later, she gave birth to a little girl named Selma Priscilla Kershaw. She was tiny, barely two pounds, and they were going to airlift her to Atlanta Children's Hospital, but Staci was thankful to God that her baby had lived through the birth. She had requested that Nocturnal not be in the delivery room. That may have been petty, but she didn't care. He was the cause of this calamity. All she wanted was to be surrounded by her children, the only ones who really loved her. It had taken her a moment to come to that realization, but she'd gotten it loud and clear. As soon as they allowed her to be discharged, she was heading to Atlanta to be with Selma and stay there for as long as it took to get her healthy.

"Staci, let me take Chauncory and Sadie home with me. They're tired and you need to rest, baby."

They were resting. They had fallen asleep in the recliner in her hospital room, sharing a pillow and blanket. Chauncory was holding his sister and both were snoring lightly.

"No, Momma, I need my babies. They're all I got and I don't want them away from me right now. I almost lost Selma, and it's possible she might not survive. And if she does, she'll have a lot of medical complications and possibly, lifelong disabilities. So, please let me just be with my children in peace."

"Staci, you're being selfish. You know Percy is out there crying his eyes out, worried about you and Selma. It broke his heart not to be here in the delivery room. He's never missed a child being born and you were wrong to treat him like that," she fussed.

"No, I wasn't. He's been cheating on me, mistreating me, and I'm done. No disrespect, Momma, but I'm not you. I'm not going to allow the father of my children to hurt and mistreat me. I told him I wanted a ring and a wedding. I needed commitment. Do you know what he did? He saw Vicious with the female he cheated on me with and got pissed about it," Staci blurted out. It hurt so bad to talk, her body ached like she was knocking on death's door, but she was so riled up and indignant that she didn't care.

"Calm down now, gal. You're running your blood pressure up for nothing. I'm on your side. I am but, baby, don't be mean just to be mean. At the end of the day, he's the father of your children and he wants to be. I had to call the white man on your daddy just to get a two-dollar child support check. You have a man who takes care of you and your children. Albeit, I don't like his illegal activity, but he's never put you and the children in danger and that counts for something."

"Momma, when he cheated on me numerous times without using protection, he put my health and the health of our children at risk. He could have given me an incurable STD. I know you're team Nocturnal, but I can't live like that anymore. The more I go to church and learn the Gospel, the more I see that he and I are unequally yoked. That's why he disrespects me and dismisses my feelings like I don't matter. He don't care about me."

"Then why do you stay?"

"Guilt, but now, it ain't even worth it. I don't even care now. He can go left."

"Guilt over what?" her mother questioned.

It was then Staci noticed that she had just said too much, but she had to tell the truth. That was part of accepting Christ. Secrets and lies needed to be confessed. "Chauncory isn't Noc's biological son. I was messing with Vicious and Noc at the same time. I didn't know who the father was until he was born, and I didn't know I was pregnant until after Vicious had been sentenced. My baby got his daddy's good grain of hair and dark eyes. He even got his daddy's personality."

"Staci, seriously?"

"Yes, I was young, stupid, and about that life. I had two of the best-looking dudes pining for my attention. It made me feel important and I believed I was that girl. I know it's messed up, but they filled that void that my father never could. I needed to feel worthy and special and they did that for me until you got saved and started getting me to go to church. Then I started to see the error of my ways, but I fought it. I've wanted to tell Nocturnal and Vicious both, but Vicious was so rude that I just couldn't tell him."

"You haven't told Nocturnal because you want the security of a marriage, but baby, that don't mean anything, he could ask for a divorce."

"It don't matter now because I'm leaving him for good this time. I'll be a mother and father to my children."

"That's not right, Staci. Oh, my goodness, that's why his name is Thesis Chauncory. Girl, that's trifling." For a moment, Sharifa was speechless and could only shake her head. "I didn't raise you that way. I'll pray for you and I hope you will listen to God. This ain't right. Secrets have a way of spilling out and it's always worse. You need to tell the truth for Chauncory's sake. I'm taking the kids home, but just know tomorrow it's going to be rough. You know Percy's momma is extra. Get your rest," her mother instructed and walked over to pick up Chauncory first and exited out the room. Then a second later, she returned for Sadie. "Percy took Chauncory to my car. That's why I came back so fast for Sadie. After church, I'm coming back to get you settled and bring stuff for you and the baby. Staci, pray and be honest. I love you, baby," she told her and kissed her cheek.

A & Ω

Nocturnal looked at his daughter. She was super tiny. He had never seen a baby so small, and it was his fault. He had stressed out Staci so badly that she'd gone into premature labor and now, she was refusing to see him. He released a hard breath. His red-rimmed eyes couldn't create another tear, but his soul was crying. "I'm sorry, Selma. I promise I'll be a better father. Your momma mad at me and rightly so, but I love you, your big brother, Chauncey, and your sister, Sadie. Everything I do, I do for all of you. You're a Kershaw, so I know you're a fighter, and I need you to fight hard baby, girl. I'ma fight too. I'ma fight for our family," he vowed.

Nocturnal wanted to stay with his daughter, but she was underdeveloped and in need of medical attention. The travel nurses were in a rush to get his daughter to safety. He did the hardest thing he'd ever had to do. He let her go.

Nocturnal had sent Congo home. How could he, the dude that ran the streets, not be able to do anything for his little girl? He felt useless and helpless. The words that Staci had spoken when they argued about not needing a baby ripped through him. He wanted his baby and he wanted his. If he lost them, then he didn't know what he'd do.

Nocturnal wasn't a good dude. He had done some horrible things in his short life. He'd committed just about every sin one could imagine and he was ignorant enough to worship himself. He had put his faith in his abilities, but he wasn't the one who had the ability to save his daughter. That was up to God, who he hadn't spoken to in years because life had made him heartless.

Nocturnal hated rules and thrived on breaking them. He was a firm believer in doing whatever made him happy until he discovered just how limited that kind of living was. God was all. He was everything and he needed God to save his daughter. She'd just been born and she was fighting to survive. It was his fault, his selfishness. He clasped his hands and dropped his head. He had no idea how to pray or what to say so he just let his tears speak on his behalf and then he left the hospital. He didn't even go see Staci. He knew she hated him right now and that was okay because he hated himself as well. Tomorrow would be better. It had to be.

Chapter 17

*V*irtuous and her family entered the church and headed to their usual pew. They'd gotten a late start, so they had missed Sunday school. Virtuous was still in awe that Jason had come to her rescue. He had never done so before and she was curious as to what had caused the change. She was thankful for his intervention.

As they were about to sit, Virtuous heard a feminine voice call Jason's name and her head snapped around. She frowned momentarily, frozen in fear. What was Maisha doing here and how did she know Jason. Furthermore, was Theory here too? This could be catastrophic if he was. She discreetly glanced around, but she didn't see him. She let out a breath she didn't know she'd been holding.

"Who is that?" Greg asked her, apparently unaffected by her reaction.

Before she could answer, Jason brought Maisha over. "Daddy, Vivi, this is my girlfriend, Maisha. Mai, this is my little sister, Vivi."

"Of course, we met at the movie theater. It's so good to see you again," Maisha said.

"Oh, you two know each other?" Jason asked, grinning. His entire demeanor had changed once Mai arrived, which warmed Virtuous' heart. Hopefully, he'd be nothing like Greg.

"Not well, we just met at the movies," Maisha explained.

All Virtuous could do was nod in agreement. Honestly, she and Maisha had hit it off well.

"Great. Come on and let's sit down. When church is over, I'll introduce you to my grandparents and other sisters," Jason told her.

Virtuous was grateful that Mai didn't out her. It was like she had sensed something was off, but she didn't speak on it. Thank God for that blessing because the last thing she needed was for Greg to become unhinged. He was every bit his name's origin. Gregory meant watchful and alert and he never missed anything even when she thought he did.

"So, that's his girlfriend. She's cute," Greg commented and motioned for Virtuous to sit down. He reached his arm around her shoulder and pulled her in. Her family, apart from the children, who were in children's church, and Tamari and her family came to sit with them.

Pastor Edwin asked for Virtuous and Greg to come forward for prayer. "Sisters and brothers, the Hartford family has been through it. I asked Greg if it would be okay to share this and he said it was. Our sister, Addison Hartford, is a recent victim among many of this opioid epidemic. It's because of that she, unfortunately, attacked her daughter, Vivi. So, family, I ask that we pray for the entire family. Lay hands of love over them as they deal with this difficult quandary," Pastor Edwin requested.

Greg reached out for Virtuous' hand and she obstinately allowed her hand in his. He was really eating up the attention. He made his eyes water knowing good and well he didn't care about Addison. He'd wanted her gone. Virtuous wanted to remove her hand from his, fearing that God would strike him down for his deceit. After Pastor Edwin was done praying, Greg asked if he could speak, which was her cue to walk away.

"First off, I just want to thank everyone for their prayers. My family has been hit hard. I tell you it's tough raising four children, but I'm so thankful for my parents and my two oldest, Jason and Vivi, for being so involved with their sisters. For so long, I tried to help my wife, but it was a struggle and I felt like a failure as a husband. It broke my heart when she didn't want me anymore. I fought for our marriage, but it was in vain. I was dealing with that as best I could, but when she..." he paused and pretended to be getting choked up and Pastor Edwin patted his back to encourage him to speak. Virtuous was livid at his acting skills and flat-out lies. "She attacked sweet Virtue. You all know Virtue's heart is pure. When Addison attacked my child, not for the first time, but the second time, I just... Lord have mercy, I just couldn't take it. I'm a firm believer in marriage and working it out until you get it right, but I can't stay married to a woman who abuses my children. I just need your continued support and prayers as I prepare my children for what's to come next. It breaks my heart, but God is good, and I know He'll see us through this," he concluded and had the nerve to cry.

"Amen, brother, we're here for you," some of the members called out. The ones near Virtuous patted her shoulders or said sweet encouragements. They incorrectly assumed her red face and watery eyes were because of what Greg had shared, but they were from what he was not saying. She was so happy he was going to be gone for his training that she didn't know what to do.

After completing his Academy Award-winning performance, he slowly traveled back to their pew, shaking hands and receiving hugs on the way. This was why she knew no one would believe he had been abusing her for years. He had these people eating out the palm of his hand. They really believed that he was the victim and not the perpetrator. By no means was Addison innocent. She was complicit and just as guilty as Greg. She had helped hide Virtuous' pregnancy. She had forged the medical documentation and she was the one who had told Greg to take her to North Carolina to give birth. Virtuous dropped her head as the old memories overtook her.

By the time Greg made his way to her she was a full-blown mess and he was made to look like the hero. He pulled her into him and whispered in her ear and stroked her back. "It's okay, baby."

"Greg, maybe you should let us take her to the bathroom to calm her down," Cate offered, as Tamari ran over.

"Okay. Virtue, Cate and Tamari are going to take you to the restroom to clean you up." Then his lips kissed her ear.

"Don't say anything stupid, Virtue," he warned before handing her off.

She finally calmed down, but she didn't return to the sanctuary. Instead, she and Tamari just hung out in one of the private rooms.

"Vivi, was that the girl we met at the movies with Jason?"

"Yes, they're dating."

"I knew Jay liked the chocolate sisters," she teased.

"I think Cary does too. He was asking me about Rika, but I think Nimo is interested in her as well."

"She's a beautiful girl, so I'm sure they both are interested."

Then silence fell between them and she knew that Tamari wanted to ask her a question. It was burning on her lips. They had talked on the phone about Theory and how she'd met him and how she had to keep it secret, but Tamari had no clue that Tory was her daughter or that Greg was abusing her.

"How do you do it?" Tamari asked.

"Do what?"

"Keep it together. I mean Addison had to attack you more than twice and I've known for a while something was off because of how you've been acting. Then you're always with your sisters like you're afraid to leave them alone. Somehow, you maintain a high grade point average and draw better than anyone I know and never complain. I don't think I could do it."

"I do it for Maddison and Tory. If not for them, I wouldn't make it either. I do get tired. I have a house to maintain, kids to raise, and all I want to do is enjoy my senior year, go out on dates with Theory, and have fun with you. But I can't. I'm a prisoner in my own life and I'm scared for anything good to come my way because I know evil will devour it."

"Vivi, I'm so sorry. I wish I could make it better for you. We'll all help. You and your dad don't have to carry the burden alone. I'll babysit for free."

"I wish that was all it was."

"Just tell me what you need me to do and I'll do it. You're my best friend. Whatever it is, just pray about it. God hears our verbal and nonverbal prayers."

"I don't think He hears mine anymore, Mari. And honestly, I'm tired of praying the same prayer."

"No, don't say that," Tamari replied softly, wrapping her arm around Virtuous. "I don't like you talking like this. It's not the Vivi I know."

"That's because that Vivi died a long time ago," she mumbled.

A & Ω

Later as Virtuous was exiting the church, Serena called out to her. "Vivi, can I speak with you for a moment?" She turned toward Greg. He had already given her an earful for not returning to the sanctuary.

"Daddy, can I go?"

"Yeah, go see what she wants and then come back. We have a reservation at the restaurant."

Virtuous nodded to him and then sauntered over to Serena. She looked extremely pretty in her lavender floral-print maxi dress. Her thick, wavy hair hung freely, kissing her cinnamon skin. She offered Virtuous an endearing smile, which she returned.

Once she made it to her, Serena wrapped her arms around her shoulders and the pair strolled together until they were away from the exiting crowd. "Vivi, you know I'm a licensed psychologist and I do a lot of trauma work and volunteer at the rape crisis center."

"Yes," she answered, unsure of why she'd stated that. She leaned her head to the side to shield her eyes from the sun and waved her arms to shoo away various insects as she patiently waited for Serena to expound.

"You know that you can come to me if you need anything, right?"

"I do." This must be about Greg's epic confession.

"Honey, you've been through a traumatic ordeal with what your mother did to you. Your grandparents and I were talking after you left service and they asked me to check in with you. I've noticed how you kind of disassociate from the world. If you need someone to listen to you, and you have my word it will remain confidential, then I'm here."

Serena had spoken so soft and hypnotically that Virtuous almost poured out her heart, almost until Greg interrupted.

"Virtue?" she heard him call.

"Thank you, Serena. I'll keep that in mind. I better go now," Virtuous replied prepared to walk to the parking lot.

"Vivi, if you need me for anything, just call me please. Anything you say to me will be protected under client-clinician privilege. I'd never betray your trust. *Never.* Before you go, let's pray."

Vivi nodded and padded back to Serena. They held hands dropped their heads and began to pray. She could hear Greg's impatient footfalls. He didn't like being made to wait, but he didn't interrupt. Once they were done praying, Greg reached out for Vivi and cupped his hand around the back of her neck as he escorted her to his truck.

A & Ω

Theory and his family had just finished church. He wanted to call Vivi, but he had to wait because her daddy was around. He was taking the family to Wade's for Sunday lunch because their food was the bomb. It was almost as good as Grammy's.

"Ri, where's Mai at?"

"She went to church with her boyfriend, Jason."

"*Jason*? Which one? Is it J-Roc, J-Boog, JJ, or Ja?" Theory asked.

"Nah, bruh, it's none of them Anderson homies. It's just plain Jason. Mai got a *white* boyfriend, not that it matters. He seems cool. There's nothing vulgar on his social media pages. He seems to like hunting and football and he attends college," Valor explained.

"What? How do you know and *I* don't when I spend more time with them than you?"

"I told you to get Instagram. He likes all her IG photos even her jacked up ones where she puts on them stupid dog ears and floral crowns and whatnot. Then she changed her relationship status on Facebook to *in a relationship*. You know when it's on Facebook it's official."

"Oh, I missed that. Ri, why didn't you tell me?"

"I'on have social media. All I'm allowed to have is Pinterest and YouVersion Bible App. Daddy said I gotta be eighteen before I can get anything else. He scared I'll get Catfished or kidnapped. He's been watching too much Web of Lies on ID. Anyhow, I just knew she was talking to someone, but she didn't share details. Besides, I got my own life," she retorted.

"Watch that sass, Rika," Theory chastised before turning to his grandmother. "Grammy, did you know about this?"

"I found out just recently. She's going to meet his family today, and next Sunday, Jason is coming to her house to meet us."

"Argh. I need to get to the hospital!" Rika exclaimed, causing everyone in the car to grow quiet.

"Why? Who got hurt?" a concerned Theory asked.

"Staci is in the hospital. She had her baby way too early. Theory, I know you don't care for her, but we should at least check on her. They airlifted her baby to Atlanta."

"You can go. I'm not stopping you, but there are two things you gotta do. One, you take someone with you and two, you stay clear of Congo. But I'ma make sure Grammy gets her something to eat first."

"Baby, I appreciate that, but I think we should check on Staci. You know she used to come by here after you got in that trouble, but then she stopped coming. I guess she thought I would judge her because she got pregnant, but it wasn't none of my business," Grammy shared.

Theory side-eyed her. He knew she had some children because her body told that story, but he didn't know she was pregnant when he got caught up. "Grammy, how many kids she got?"

"Well, counting this one, I believe it's three. Isn't that right, Ri?"

Theory looked in the review mirror and noticed that his cousin was acting strange, but she kept her eyes on her cellphone. "Yes, it's three with this baby."

"How old?" Theory was pretty sure she was messing around with him and Noc at the same time and if so, she was lower than a snake for that.

"I don't know," Rika told him.

"Valor, do you?" he noticed how quiet his cousin had become and that wasn't Val. That indicated he knew something.

"From what I ascertained, she was unfaithful while the two of you were together and she got pregnant by Nocturnal. Her son is or about to be five and the little girl is three."

"Right, that was exactly what I was thinking." Theory shook his head. He knew she had snake tendencies. He let it go. Staci was no longer his concern and he didn't care. "So, um, y'all wanna get KFC and then head up the road or call an order into Wade's?"

"I want Wade's," Val declared.

"Yeah, just do that and then we can link up with Mai and go."

"You can meet Mai. I'm not going," Theory corrected.

A & Ω

Staci felt like crap. Out of all her childbirths, this one was the worse physically and emotionally. She was depleted and then some. It had been a long day already and it was only a little past noon. As soon as she got up, she requested for only certain people to be allowed to see her because she didn't want to be bothered. She just wanted to be discharged and go to her daughter.

Letting out a sigh, she closed her eyes. It seemed like a moment, but she was sure it had been longer because when a voice interrupted her, she felt herself waking from a slumber she didn't know she was under.

"Staci, are you sleeping?"

Staci's body chilled at the sound of his voice. Hearing him grated her nerves. She had nothing to say to Nocturnal. Her anger and hurt were still fresh. "Leave now, Percival. There's no reason for you to be in my room. You aren't welcome in here to see or speak to me. I'm sure your trollop, Lourdes, is around, so go talk to her."

"Stop acting so callous and ridiculous. Nobody's thinking 'bout that girl. You're being super petty and you got yo cousins banging on the door talkin' 'bout they were supposed to move you out."

"And?"

"And, you know that's childish. The last time you moved and took my kids from me was the *last time*. It's not going to be a get mad at me and then take the kids. That's psychotic and dysfunctional."

Before she could reply there was a knock on the door followed by a greeting. She knew those voices. "Hey, Maisha and Rika. Y'all, c'mon in."

"We brought Grammy too. She wanted to see you," Maisha stated, bringing in balloons, a card, a teddy bear, and a gift bag. "We didn't get to have your baby shower, but we got a little something," Mai spoke for the group as they all nodded to Nocturnal.

"Get comfortable, y'all. Noc was just leaving, but my momma is bringing Sadie and Chauncory over. She just left to get me some Chick-fil-A," she told them, completely ignoring Nocturnal.

"Excuse me, y'all," Noc interrupted. Then he gave Staci an ugly glare before leaving.

Staci didn't care. He had started it and she was finishing it.

Chapter 18

Greg blinked his eyes hard. This training was good, but it was tiresome, and he was concerned about his family. Surprisingly, he hadn't heard from Addison, at least not directly. Her father, Tommy had phoned him and asked him to drop the charges because she was entering rehab and her reaction had been drug induced. Greg had explained that he had no control over that. They could petition the court, but his hands were tied. That had pissed her father off, but he didn't care. Addison had gone too far, and he wasn't going to rescue her this time. He and Addison were now legally separated and after a year, he would be able to divorce her. He had proof that Addison had been unfaithful.

All he wanted was to end that part of his life and start his new life with Virtue. Her change in demeanor upset him. Virtue was starting to express herself in a way he couldn't comprehend. He needed her to be that insecure, scared, submissive girl she used to be. He blamed his meddling mother and sister-in-law, Cate, who were constantly telling him that Virtue needed to go out more with her peers.

"Greg, are you okay?" Montez, Tamari's father, asked.

"Yeah, just thinking about the family."

"Sorry about that, man," Montez offered and placed a reassuring pat on his shoulder. "At least the kids are doing well. Vivi is about to graduate and that's great considering what you all have been through."

He nodded. "Mo, has Tamari said anything to you about Virtue and Nimo. You know, like, are they dating?"

"No, but if that were the case, I figured you'd know first. You're the one working with the kids. At least Nimo has a good head on his shoulders and he's an excellent quarterback. I can't believe our baby girls are old enough to be dating."

"Well, Vivi isn't allowed to date."

Montez guffawed. "That's what you think. These days our kids can have an entire relationship and parents will never know. Technology is the devil. These kids got apps that hide all their activity and iPhones help them keep secrets. So, I just accept it and keep an open line of communication. Vivi is a good kid and she's responsible, so I think you should let her out more. Either that, or she'll start sneaking around," Montez warned.

That didn't sit well with Greg. In fact, it upset him more than he cared to admit, but before he could reply, his cell started to ring. He excused himself and answered in private. "Dad, is everything okay? Are the girls good?"

"The girls are fine, Greg. Are you coming home this weekend or just staying till the training is over?"

"I was planning on staying, but I just had a conversation with Montez and it concerned me. Let me talk to Virtue."

"She's not here."

"Where is she?"

"She's taking Maddison over to Cate."

"Oh... Well, how's she been this week?"

"Greg, she's fine. Just like when you asked before. She's been on her phone a lot and drawing, spending time with her friends. Son, I was wondering why Tory calls Vivi *Mama*, Greg?"

"Dad, I have to go. They're calling me back. I'll call later. Make sure you tell Virtue to call me." He hung up.

A & Ω

Nocturnal hadn't gotten any sleep. His family was separated once again and that disturbed him on many levels, and Lourdes acted like she had an attitude. Currently, Staci was down in Atlanta with the baby. After she was discharged without notifying him, she went to their home, took her clothes and the kids' clothes, and left town, headed to Atlanta. The only reason Chauncey was in South Carolina was that he had school, but Staci had taken Sadie with her. She had ticked him off so badly that he wanted to take the engagement ring back he'd bought her. She was cutting all the way up. Then when he called her, she had their daughter answer. Like, how was *Sadie* going to give him updates on Selma? He had to call the doctors directly.

"Chauncey, what's wrong with you?" His son had been acting funny lately. He didn't know if it was because his momma and sister were gone or because he could sense something going on between him and Staci.

"I'm mad!" Chauncey fussed, causing Noc to lift his brow in concern.

"You're mad about what and who are you snapping at like that, lil'dude?"

"I'm mad at you because you made momma cry and you made her leave. I wanna go to Granny Sharifa's house," he fussed and crossed his arms and glared at Noc through the review mirror.

For a moment, Nocturnal had to remember that this was his five-year old son and not some knucklehead in the street. He pulled his car into the barbershop parking lot because this needed to be settled before he took his son down to Atlanta to visit his momma and sisters. His son was getting removed from that white afterschool program today, 'cause only white kids talked to their parents like that. He got out of the car and opened the back seat and got him.

"Chauncey, what did you say to me?"

"I said you made my mommy cry. You made her leave. I'm mad at you. I want my Granny," he spoke clearly and showed no fear.

Then he had the nerve to curl his lips like he was somebody. His boy had heart, but he was barking up the wrong tree. "Son, I'm your father and you don't talk to me like that."

"Nuh-uh, you're not my daddy!"

"What?"

"You're not my daddy. Mommy said so," he enunciated each word like he was a speech therapist.

Nocturnal had to get out of the car and he slammed the door. He stomped off and reminded himself that his son was five and that jacking him up in public was a bad idea.

He could deal with a lot, but Staci had gone too far with this one. He took three deep breaths, headed back to the car, and then opened the door. "Chauncey, I know you're upset with me about your momma leaving, but she had to go to be with Selma. She didn't leave you and I didn't make her cry. She's sad about your little sister. Okay?"

Chauncey didn't speak. He just stared at Nocturnal with big rustic eyes. "It's not nice to say I'm not your dad because I *am*. I love you, your sisters, and your momma. She probably said that, but she didn't mean it."

"She *did* say it," the child confirmed.

"She shouldn't have said that because it's not true. Staci can be mean when she's hurt and upset, okay."

"You're my daddy then?"

"Yeah, son, I'm your daddy. Now, let's get ready to head down to Atlanta to see your momma and sisters."

As Noc got back into the driver's side, his mind kept replaying what his son had said. He wasn't his father. Nocturnal just couldn't shake it. He waited until son went to sleep. It was a two-hour drive to Atlanta. They had another hour to go. He picked up his cellphone and dialed Staci. If she put his daughter on the phone to avoid him, he was going choke her out.

"Hello?" came a gruff voice, it sounded like she had just woken up, but he didn't care. He was livid.

"So, I'm not Chauncey's father?"

"What?" she screeched. "I-I-I'm sorry."

"Oh, now you wanna play apologetic? You know he heard you talking to probably your messy sister, Jenna, claiming I wasn't his father. He said that I made you cry, and I made you leave. Staci, I know you pissed about the way I handled the Lourdes incident, but don't you *ever* tell my children I ain't their daddy. You went too far, Staci, but I'll chalk that up to you being overly emotional because our daughter is fighting for her life. We're even now, but that's the last slide you get. Act a fool again, play with me if you wanna and I swear you'll see another side of me." He hung up on her.

A & Ω

Theory rang the doorbell at Vi's grandparents' house and waited for someone to answer. He was grinning all over himself. Ever since Greg had left for his two-week training, Theory and Virtuous had spent every day together. He'd get off work and drive to Boiling Springs, and just hang out at the organic food store that her grandparents owned or they'd take a drive, sometimes with her sister and daughter and sometimes just the two of them. He had become completely enamored with her. She was quiet and soft spoken, but she was also strong and resilient. It made her insanely beautiful. He and Jason had even become cool. Now, all he had to do was help Vivi find the courage to tell her family all the terrible secrets so she could be free. She had told him numerous times that she didn't think the police would act or believe her because Greg was the police and she felt stuck.

"Hey, Theory, we're ready. Maddison is with Cate, but she made you this picture and she said she was sad she couldn't see you today," Virtuous told him as she handed him a picture that the child had drawn.

"She's too good to me. Are you ready?" He had finally convinced her to meet his family. He talked about her so much that everyone wanted to officially meet her, even Shalamar. They were having another epic cookout.

"Yes, I'm ready. Please get Tory and her diaper bag. I made several desserts and I need to get them. Tory's extra car seat is seating on the rocking chair." He nodded at her instructions. He was used to this. Tory came to him eagerly, speaking her baby English and kissing his cheeks. She was a super cute baby and easy to love. When they'd gone to Walmart earlier in the week, he'd gotten stopped like five times because people were so taken by her beauty. Tory looked just like her momma, a carbon copy, so it puzzled him how her family didn't see the resemblance or maybe they didn't want to see it.

By the time he got Tory settled, Vivi came out of the house followed by her grandmother, carrying a butt load of cakes, pies, and cupcakes.

"Dang, Proverbs, did you spend all last night baking?" He reached for the sweet treats to put them neatly in his truck.

"Mamaw helped me. I just wanted to make a good impression."

"They like you already," he assured her. Proverbs could cook like she made him a feast for dinner last night. He told her that he liked country-fried steak and she did her thing. The food alone had him ready to wife her up. Seventeen-year-old girls didn't cook like that.

"Mrs. Hartford, I'll have your girls back at a respectable hour."

"I know you will. Maybe you can come back a little early, so Maddison can see you. All my granddaughters are smittened with you, Theo," she cooed.

"It's the Campbell charm," he teased. Yup, Mamaw loved him too. Now, her grandfather was a different matter, but Theory didn't care. He had yet to meet Norman or Cate.

"I believe it. You all have a good time and I'll see y'all later," LeAnn answered as she watched them get ready to leave.

Theory opened the door for Virtuous and once she was secured inside, he shut the door and then jogged to his side of the truck. Once he got in, he opened the dashboard and pulled out a neatly wrapped rectangle box and sat it on Virtuous' lap. "I got you a little something."

"That's sweet, Theory, but you didn't have to do that. Did you get me these because I bought you that book set of James Baldwin reads?"

"No, Proverbs, I got you that because you deserve it, but I do love my book collection," he told her as he started to play Alessia Cara who was Vivi's favorite pop singer. He'd been playing it ever since he'd started riding with her and she had it on nonstop.

Theory put the truck in drive and heard Vivi unwrap her gift. She didn't even know what it was and was already smiling. That was what he liked about her. She took nothing for granted and appreciated everything no matter how small.

"I hope you like it."

Once she opened it completely, she gasped. "Theory, this is so beautiful. I've never had real jewelry before. Thank you. I love it," she cooed, gently removing the gold eighteen karat charm bracelet from the box. It had a Bible hanging with Proverbs 31 inscribed on it. There was also a paint brush charm because she loved art and the letter T for his initial. There were two little girls, one Maddison and the other Tory. He wanted to make them official, but he wasn't sure how to broach the subject.

"Good, Mai helped me with the charms."

"This is so perfect. Everything that is important to me is on here. You're so thoughtful, Theory."

"I try." He was about to say more when his ringing cellphone interrupted them. He didn't like to talk on his phone and drive, so he'd had a new system installed in his truck that had Bluetooth capability. The only thing was he didn't recognize the number but answered anyway.

"Who is this?"

"Vicious, it's Staci."

"How did you get my number and why are you contacting me?" He was baffled. He side-eyed Virtuous, but she was still admiring her gift and taking a picture of it with her phone.

"I need to have a serious conversation with you. I'm down in Atlanta caring for my premature daughter, but when I get back to town we need to talk."

"No. We've been done, and I got nothing to say to you. I'm about to hang up."

"Why, because that tramp is with you? Mm, you too good to speak to me now because you're messing around with

Lourdes? I hope you know she's using you to make Noc jealous."

That statement got a reaction out of Virtuous, who was now fully tuned into the conversation and giving him a fiery glare. Theory didn't have to pivot his head to verify that. He could feel the flames.

"Staci, get off my line with your lies."

"Oh, I see. You must have your little white girl with you. I guess she don't know about that Saturday when—"

Theory clicked her off. Staci had some nerve to call him on that foolishness. He was going to see her again. Then he looked over at Virtuous who had turned a few shades of red and not the cute blush that he was accustomed to seeing. No, this was pissed-off red. He silently berated himself for even answering the phone call. "Proverbs, it's not like she's making it sound," he defended.

"It sounds like you lied to me. You said you were hanging out with your friend, Archie, and if I needed you, I could call. What you failed to inform me about was Lourdes, your date. Who is Staci? You know what? It's cool. Just take me home."

Theory had to look at her twice because the Virtuous he knew didn't talk like that or at least, she'd never spoken to him like that before. Her tone was cold. It took him aback a moment. She was picking up some of Maisha's traits. Once he got over the initial shock of her response, he spoke. "No, let me explain before you get mad for nothing."

"Take me home, Theory." Her voice was coarse and filled with emotion

"Why? This is absurd. I'm not taking you home just yet. Listen, I went out with Archie and his friend, Yulonda, because he had asked me to be his wingman. Yulonda's friend, Lourdes, was in town. I explained to her that I had a girl and that I was simply there as a favor to my friend. She was cool. Then after we ate, we ran into my past. There's a lot I didn't tell you about my life prior to being in juvie because it doesn't matter. Anyway, Staci my ex from years ago arrived with her crew and apparently, the guy she had cheated on me with, Nocturnal, had a relationship with Lourdes. Now, they think that I'm with her but I'm not." he explained.

"You should have told me because now, it looks like you have something to hide. Who is the white girl she referenced?"

Theory chuckled. "That'd be you. Nora Jean ran her mouth when she saw us together at Texas Roadhouse. She incorrectly thought you were white. Look, Virtuous, real talk, I haven't had a girlfriend since I was fifteen. Even though I'm twenty-one now, I'm inexperienced in relationships, but I like you a lot and I want you to be my girl so don't let this issue that's really a misunderstanding cause you to pull away from me. I like where we are going."

Virtuous sucked on her bottom lip as she contemplated his words. "Don't hurt me, Theory. I've suffered enough."

"Baby, I swear on all that I am I'd never hurt you at least not intentionally. All I want to be is the man that makes you feel safe. Do you believe that? Do you trust me with your heart and with Tory?"

"I–I trust you."

"So, does that mean you're my girl?"

He saw a smirk graze her face. "Yes."

"Thank you, Jesus. You had ya boy nervous for a minute. Do you still want me to take you home?"

"No."

"Good, 'cause I wasn't." Theory winked and reached out for her hand and brought it to his lips.

A & Ω

As they arrived at Theory's grandmother's house, Virtuous was taken aback by the number of people. Her mind was still replaying the conversation she'd overheard and the one they had. He wanted her and her baby. That was huge. She wanted him too, but she was afraid but not of him. She was sure that Theory was trustworthy, but she was afraid of what to do when Greg returned home. He was not going to accept her being with someone else, and she was tired of his abuse, so that left one option—run away. Tory was her daughter and she had a right to protect her child at all cost.

"Don't be nervous, Proverbs. My family and friends are cool. If you feel uncomfortable at any time, just grab my hand and let me know."

Virtuous nodded, but it wasn't his family she was concerned about. Besides, she knew that Jason was here as well or on his way. She heard Theory call out to his friends to help unload the desserts she'd made. They scurried off the porch and trotted over to be of assistance.

Virtuous remembered Archie and assumed the girl with him was Yulonda. Shalamar introduced himself and behind him was the cutest pit bull puppy that she knew was named Logic. He was adorable.

Virtuous bent down to greet the little black pup and played with him for a few when she noticed someone else approaching. He was someone she hadn't met yet because Theory was trying to get her attention to introduce her. She stood back up to greet the newcomer but was shocked to silence when she saw the male version of herself. All her life she had waited for this moment and now that it was here, she thought she was seeing a mirage. "Valor?" That was the last word she spoke before she collapsed into nothingness. Her *World of All* was ending.

To be continued... Up next A Virtuous Theory (book 2)

About Y. Deonna

Y. Deonna is a native of South Carolina. At an early age she discovered her love of reading and writing. As a youngster, she was fascinated by how authors created exciting and uplifting stories and knew she would one day do the same.

It is her desire to fuse together her education, faith, and advocacy to create empowering stories that engage and educate readers. Writing Christian Fiction novels are part of her ministry and advocacy.

After the successful debut of her first novel, Deception Has A Name, and several others, Y. Deonna decided to challenge herself even more. In 2018, she founded Crown Ruby Publishing & Literary Services. Additionally, she is a Victim Advocate and works with domestic violence and sexual assault survivors.